MOON DRAGON

/ / / /

J.R. RAIN

THE VAMPIRE FOR HIRE SERIES

Published by
Crop Circle Books
212 Third Crater, Moon

Printed in the United States of America.

ISBN-13: 978-1974583300
ISBN-10: 1974583309

Dedication
To Abraham.

Acknowledgment
A special thank you to the beautiful and talented,
Diane Arkenstone.

"Here be dragons."
The Lenox Globe, circa 1510

"It is a rare vampire who can transform himself into something greater. It is an even rarer vampire who can control the demon within."
Diary of the Undead

1.

Last night, *Sixty Minutes* ran a segment on Judge Judy, which I made a point to record.

Now, with a pile of clean laundry in front of me and a pair of Anthony's briefs momentarily forgotten over one shoulder—a pair I had dubbed "The Forever Stain"—I sat, transfixed, for the entire segment.

I watched Judge Judy's rise from a small New Jersey Family Appellate Court judge to one of the highest-paid TV personalities today. *The* highest-paid part surprised me. Then again, I think she deserves every penny. After all, she is a role model for many, and the voice of reason to all. Anyway, the segment showed a softer side of the judge, and I appreciated seeing that. I like her softer side. She is a mother and grandmother. Someday, I hope to be a grandmother, too.

That I would be the world's youngest-looking grandmother was another story. That my granddaughters or grandsons would, within a few decades, look older than me, was...well, the same story. That I might never meet them was too heartbreaking to consider. Perhaps I would be introduced as a long-lost aunt or something.

I sighed when the segment was over. The judge has a beautiful life, a challenging job, and grandkids everywhere. She has aged gracefully, seemingly stronger now than ever.

Myself, I have been a vampire now for nine years. I had been turned in my late twenties. Twenty-eight, in fact. I still looked twenty-eight, perhaps even younger. Perhaps closer to twenty-five or twenty-six. I should be on the cusp of looking like I was forty. Instead, I look like I am a few years out of grad school.

I might look young. I might have the strength of ten women. I might even occasionally turn into a giant vampire bat. But raising two kids—one of whom was a teenager and the other was damn close —seriously took a superhuman effort. How mortals did it, I would never know.

I sighed heavily when I turned off the TV, briefly jealous of the life Judge Judy had created, and wondering how the hell my life was going to turn out, knowing I would have to cross that bridge when I got there.

My doorbell rang.

I looked at the time on my cell. My potential client was early.

I glanced at the laundry piles scattered over the couch and recliner and shrugged. That's what my potential client got for being early. Still, I quickly shoved the briefs under the biggest pile. No one deserved to see The Forever Stain. Even early clients. Hell, even my worst enemies. Truly cruel and unusual punishment.

I had long since ditched my annoying habit of reaching up for my sunglasses every time I opened the front door, or checking my exposed skin for sunblock. Indeed, those habits had been eradicated in this past year. A year I had spent "living in the light," as Allison liked to put it. *Allison is annoying too, but I love her.*

Now, I confidently opened the front door and ushered in a woman I knew. A woman I loathed. A woman I nearly slammed the front door on, or tripped as she came in. Or blindsided and tackled her to the floor where I wanted to give her the world's biggest noogie and wedgie and then drag her over to my bathroom toilet for a "swirlie," as the kids used to call it back when I was in high school.

But I didn't.

I had been preparing myself all day to see Nancy Pearson. Or, as she liked to be called in a former life, Sugar Pearson.

She was, of course, the woman my murdered

ex-husband had cheated on me with while we were married. She had called earlier today and requested to see me. I had nearly told her to go to hell. In fact, I was fairly certain I had thought it loud enough for her to hear it, because she had said, "Excuse me" at one point.

Anyway, she needed help and thought I was the right woman for the job.

Oh, joy.

So, being the sucker that I am—or, as Kingsley puts it, the bleeding heart that I am—I allowed the woman into my home, the woman who'd helped to destroy my marriage. I led her down the hall and into my office.

I settled behind my desk, and she did the same in front of my desk, in one of the three client chairs.

"So," I said, noticing my heartbeat had picked up its pace, which, for me, was saying something. I also noted that my inner alarm system was ringing slightly just inside my ear. "Talk."

She nodded, took in some air and tried to look me in the eye, gave up, and finally looked away. "I'm fairly certain—no, scratch that—I'm most definitely certain, that my ex-boyfriend is a serial killer."

2.

Her aura glowed a light blue.

She was telling the truth, and yet my warning system was still chiming slightly. I've learned to listen to this warning system. The problem was, well, it wasn't precise. I didn't know exactly *why* it was ringing, only that something about this woman presented a threat to me.

I thought about that when I said, "Why not go to the police?"

"I can't prove anything."

"Then how do you know?"

The girl with the stage name of "Sugar," but whose real name was Nancy Pearson, was having a hard time sitting still. She crossed and recrossed her legs in, let's admit it, a fabulous display of dexterity. I could see how someone as feeble-minded as Danny would get seduced by such athleticism. She had probably worked the stripper stage impressively. None of which made me like her any better. Now, her high-heeled foot jiggled and bounced hyperactively. She looked like a woman with a secret, or someone who had to pee, or...

"Do you mind if I smoke?"

"I do."

"Seriously?" she said.

"Seriously," I said.

"Please?"

"No."

"Pretty please?"

"Okay."

"Really?"

"No."

"You're mean."

"You have no idea. Now talk."

She took out her packet of cigarettes anyway, opened it, removed a slightly bent one, stuck it between her teeth, and said, "Then let me at least pretend."

"Pretend all you want."

She did just that, sucking on the end of it like a real pro. She even exhaled. She did this again and I tried not to laugh.

"It's not funny," she said.

"I tried not to laugh."

"Well, you didn't do a very good job of it."

I waited as she inhaled again on her unlit cigarette, exhaled some nonexistent smoke. Her foot bounced at the end of her ankle like a fish dangling from a line. Then, she actually asked for an ashtray.

"There are no ashes," I pointed out reasonably.

"Please," she said. "It helps."

I sighed and rooted around a bottom drawer and found something Anthony had made back in arts and crafts when he was in first grade. I use the words "arts and crafts" liberally. Whatever it was— a hand or a butt cheek—I set it in front of her. She shrugged and proceeded to tap off some invisible ashes.

Our last encounter was a memorable one. Sugar had tried to stop me as I approached my then-husband's office. Tried being the operative word. I might have hit her hard enough to break her nose. And I might have enjoyed it way too much.

"I said sorry about that," said Sugar. She had picked up on my thoughts and assumed, like most people did, that I had spoken. I had not. And, yes, earlier on the phone, she had apologized again about sleeping with Danny.

"So you said."

"I mean, you aren't still mad about that, are you? That was, like, years ago."

"Two and a half years ago. And, yes, I'm still mad."

"Well, I'm sorry. If it wasn't me, it would have been any of the other girls. Your husband was, like, into all of us."

"Good to know."

"Besides, I haven't seen him in, like, over a year. Have you?"

"On and off," I said, referring to his ghost who appeared occasionally in my home. I usually found him in the kid's rooms, standing over them as they slept. Sugar didn't need to know that Danny had been murdered by a vampire who had been out to get me, too. Or that Danny had aligned with the wrong team...and had gotten himself killed. Which is why I blocked those thoughts.

She said, "Okay, well, tell him I miss him."

And I saw it there, on her face, and heard it in her voice. She truly had feelings for him. Sadly, I didn't miss him so much. Rarely, in fact. Perhaps only once or twice, tops. Not like the kids, who still mourn for their daddy. At least someone had loved Danny before he died, because it sure as hell wasn't me.

"I'll tell him," I said, and my voice might have softened a bit, dammit. Yeah, I have a bleeding heart for sure. "Now, why do you think your ex-boyfriend is a serial killer?"

She picked up the unlit cigarette and held it loosely between her fingers. "Because he told me."

3.

"And why would he do that?" I asked.

Yes, she looked ridiculous with the unlit cigarette hanging from her lips. Admittedly, I admired her commitment to her habit, unhealthy as it was. I decided not to let her know that, I, too, smoked from time to time, but never in the house. Usually in the car or on long stakeouts. Even if cancerous cells did develop in my lungs, the vampire in me eradicated them instantly.

There were benefits to being what I was. And these days, now that I could go into the sun and eat and drink and be merry, the benefits far outweighed the risks.

"He talks in his sleep," said Nancy.

"And this was recently?"

"Yes."

The word *slut* might have slipped through my mind, although I wasn't one to judge. I'd had two relationships since my divorce from Danny, and three, if you counted my mental relationship with Fang, which I kinda did.

"You don't like me very much, do you?" asked Nancy. Oops, the "slut" part might have slipped out. Might have.

"No," I said. "Not really."

"You're probably wondering why I came to you and not, say, another detective."

"The thought occurred to me."

Yes, I could probe her mind for the answers I wanted. The thing was, I didn't *want* to probe her mind. I didn't *want* to dip down into her thoughts and see what made this woman tick. I also didn't want to stumble across any memories of her and Danny. At present, such memories were probably brewing on the surface...all of their lies and deception and sneaking around and not-very-good-sneaking around.

"Danny talked, too," she said, looking away.

"Not in his sleep," I said.

"No, never in his sleep. I guess we both know that." She laughed at that and kicked her leg a little; we were just two girls sharing memories of the same man in bed. A man she had taken from me, although he went willingly enough. Actually, I imagined him running from me. Turned out his instincts were partly true. Had Danny and I continued to sleep together, he would have been bonded to me as a sort of sex slave, as had been the case with Russell. I shuddered at the thought.

"Danny would tell me things," she said, sucking ridiculously at the end of the unlit cigarette and blowing out her pretend smoke. I wondered if she was even aware that the fag wasn't lit. *Yes, I'm channeling my inner Brit.*

"What things?" I asked. My eyes might have narrowed suspiciously.

She took the cigarette out of her mouth and looked at it, wrinkling her nose. Then looked me directly in the eye. "He said you're a vampire."

"Did he now?"

She nodded vigorously. "And he was scared of you. Like, irrationally scared of you."

"Because I was a vampire?"

"That's what he said."

"And did you believe him?"

"I really, really want to light this cigarette," she said.

Suddenly, I wanted one, too. I stood and said, "Follow me."

4.

We were in my back yard, smoking.

We sat side by side on the broken cement stairs that led from the kitchen down into my back yard. Despite being broken, the stairs sported a coat of gray paint. That had been Danny's answer to all of our home improvement needs: paint the crap out of it.

One of us was smoking because she had an addiction. The other was smoking because she still had a need to feel normal. There was a chance I was the latter. Of course, the entity inside me wanted nothing to do with normal.

The entity inside me could go to hell.

"I'm sorry for what I did," said Nancy, aka Sugar.

I inhaled, peering through the smoke rising before me, obscuring the neon Pep Boys' sign that itself rose above my backyard fence. Yes, I shared a backyard fence with the Pep Boys' parking lot. Handy for when I needed an emergency fuel filter. Danny did get one thing right: he got us a big back yard, which had proved to be kinda fun, back when we were a real family.

We're still a family, I thought, *just minus the Danny part.*

Of course, Danny still came around, just minus the body part. In fact, he came around more in death than he did when alive. Funny how being dead made him a more attentive father. Better late than never.

"Did you say something?" asked Nancy.

Oops. Sometimes, despite my best efforts, my thoughts leaked out, especially when I was bonding with someone.

Oh, bloody hell, I thought. *Please don't tell me I'm bonding with her.*

"I'm not that bad," said Nancy, inhaling and looking around. "And who are you talking to?"

"Sorry," I said, inhaling deeply on my own cig. "I do that sometimes."

"Do what?"

"Think out loud."

She giggled. "So do I!"

Great.

I sighed and looked at her and exhaled a plume of smoke in her direction. I had been tempted to do so in her face, but realized the longer I was with her, the more my hate for her was quickly ebbing. Above, a seagull squawked. I was fifteen miles from the sea. This time, I kept my thoughts purposely open.

"Maybe it's lost," said Nancy. "Wait a second...your lips didn't move."

"No."

"But I heard you..."

"Oh?"

She thought about that. "Actually, I heard you directly in my head. Just inside my ear."

"How cool is that?"

"I...I'm not sure it's cool. How come you aren't blinking?"

"I don't need to blink," I said.

"Oh, Jesus."

"He might have blinked," I said. "But then again, I'm not an historian."

"Then it's true," said Nancy.

"That I'm not an expert on Jesus."

She slapped my arm, a gesture that surprised both of us. "Oh, shit," she said. "Sorry."

"It's okay."

"You really are a vampire."

"I'm something that has vampiric traits," I said. The suggestion always rankled me, although, to be honest, few people suggested it. "What, exactly, I am is open to interpretation."

"You're not going to, like, kill me, are you?"

"Only if you sleep with my next husband."

"I'm really sorry about that."

I nodded toward my house. "You didn't sound sorry earlier."

"I guess I was feeling a bit defensive...and didn't think about your feelings." She made a small face at the word *feelings*. Speaking of feelings, I had a strong feeling that Nancy didn't much like talking about her own.

"And how do you think I feel?" I asked.

She scrunched up her face at the question, as if she'd bitten into a sour grape. "Well, it's like...I can feel how you felt. It's weird."

"Go on."

"You felt abandoned. Alone. Jealous. Scared. Heartbroken. And I..."

"And you what?"

"And I contributed to a lot of that."

We were silent some more, each sucking and puffing and sitting closer than I ever thought I would sit next to my ex-husband's mistress.

After a moment, she said, "It's no secret that I was a stripper. And when Danny showed an interest in me...I mean, he was a lawyer, for Christ's sake."

"You couldn't help yourself," I said.

She shrugged and I sensed her getting defensive, so I mentally pushed her to continue. If anything, hearing her side helped me to heal a little. Helped me understand a little more, too. Danny was a shit, but I had been in love with him and his actions back then had been a dagger to the heart. Mercifully, not a silver dagger.

"I had a rough life," she went on. "I'd been turning tricks since I was fifteen, after I left home."

Despite my best efforts to shield myself from her own memories, I saw them now, flashing through her mind, each more disturbing than the next. She had been abused by her parents and grandparents. Her memories made me want to never let my kids leave the house again.

"How did a hooker..." My voice trailed off.

"Go on, you can say it."

"Fine. How did a former hooker end up as Danny's legal secretary?"

"I have a funny how-we-met story." She paused. "I had a car wreck when I was hit by a drunk driver on the way home from the strip club. I had to be cut out of my car with the Jaws of Life and Danny was there when they took me to the hospital."

"Let me guess. He wanted to take your case on contingency."

"Yeah, how did you know?"

"Lucky guess. Did someone rich hit your car?"

She nodded. "I was hit by a local politician who desperately wanted to settle out of court. Danny told me that during the case, I couldn't work as a dancer, since we were claiming disability, so he gave me a little job as his legal secretary at one-tenth of what I made before, you know, to show that I had lost earning power." She paused. "Danny got me a nice out-of-court settlement and he used his part of the proceeds to buy out the strip club where I worked because I told him it was a gold mine. I used my part of the settlement to get a little condo in Beverly Hills. I went back to dancing at the club he now owned and the rest is history."

Now the pieces were coming together about why Danny had left lawyering to own a strip club. I tried not to let my eyebrows go up. "And you and Danny got pretty close, I guess," I said, not bothering to hide my irritation.

She shrugged. "Danny seemed like he liked me. And he told me he was getting a divorce from you, and that you were this horrible person. He made me not like you in return. And then..."

"And then he told you about me being a vampire."

"Yeah."

"What did you think about that?"

She looked at me long and steady before she replied, "Let's just say that I wasn't as weirded out by it as you might think."

What I saw next in her mind made me gasp. I snapped my head around and stared at her. "Your ex-boyfriend..."

"Is not so different from you, Sam..."

5.

Allison and I were at a place called Alicia's in Brea.

Besides being a typical sit-down café, Alicia's specialized in, of all adorable things, making to-go picnic lunches, complete with wicker baskets, silverware and checkered tablecloths. A picnic with Kingsley sounded like fun, now that I no longer shrank away from the light of day like a monster in a 1930s' horror movie. Maybe we could go to Tri-City Lake. Spread out a blanket in the shade. Lots of wine. And lots of canoodling—

"Canoodling?" said Allison. "Are you sure you aren't, say, a hundred and five?"

"A hundred and five?"

"It was the first number that popped into my

head."

"Oddly specific."

Allison shrugged and bit into her smoked roast beef and raspberry jelly sandwich on, of course, a slender baguette. And because I regularly fed on her —which not only enhanced my strength but also increased her own witchy powers—Allison and I also had the closest of all telepathic links.

She seemed to revel in that. Me, not so much. Luckily, she and I had become best friends—and yes, to my extreme annoyance, she even used the word "besties." Anyway, Allison had proven herself as a good and loyal friend, and a steady source of blood. Yeah, our relationship was...unorthodox. But we both benefited. Symbiosis at its best.

Except for the "bestie" part, of course. In fact, I might be the only bloodsucker on earth who has a bestie.

My life, I thought.

"Quit bitching," said Allison between bites. "You should be so lucky. I happen to come in handy."

The next thought that crossed my mind, I regretted, but there it was, and she picked up on it instantly.

"And I am not needy, Samantha Moon. I have a full, rich life, of which you should be honored to be a part."

"Oh, brother."

"Well, you should."

"Fine," I said, picking up my own sandwich.

"I'm honored as hell."

"Don't patronize me..."

It went on like this throughout the next five minutes, all while I ate the first half of my sandwich. It had been over a year since I had been given the gift of food and sunlight, thanks to two special rings, one on each hand. The rings had done much to give me back my life. Eating lunch in the light of day with my friend was a gift beyond measure.

"Okay, that's more like it," said Allison, beaming.

"Happy?" I said.

"Oh, yes," she said. "Now tell me about Nancy Home Wrecker."

"Nancy Pearson," I said. "And she's not that bad."

"Not that bad? Didn't she steal your husband and ruin your life?"

"A lot of things contributed to ruining my life. And he was on his way out anyway."

"That's a lame excuse, Sam."

"Well, the guy is dead, and what happened can't be changed...and, well, it turns out she's not that bad."

Allison, who always got a bit jealous over my other friends, set her fork down. "I thought you were going to tell me about her sadistic ex-boyfriend, not that she *wasn't that bad*."

She rattled on like this for the next few minutes, all while I consumed the second half of my sandwich. When Allison was done ranting and raving, and when I had convinced her that no one would be replacing her "bestie" status anytime soon —which seemed to mollify her—I told her what I'd learned about Nancy's ex-boyfriend.

"A werewolf?" said Allison, perhaps a little too loudly.

I shushed her. "Yes."

"Have you talked to Kingsley about him?"

"I will soon," I said. "He had a lunch meeting today."

"So, I was your second choice?" asked Allison.

"You're in rare needy form today," I said.

"I'm not nee—" She paused. "Okay, maybe a little. What can I say? You either love me or leave me."

"I love you," I said. "For now."

She stuck out her tongue at me as the waitress came by and cleared our table. I enjoyed everything about going out to eat. I treasured the small moments, even the waitress clearing the table, asking if I wanted a refill on my iced tea. I just loved it all. I loved the chatter of women from a nearby table; they were insurance adjusters from the nearby Mercury Insurance office. One of them kept glancing at me, a tall redhead who reminded me of Nicole Kidman. Some people sense I am different; some people have enhanced psychic abilities. They may not understand why I am different, but they feel it, and give me strange looks. Like the redhead just now. I smiled at her. She blushed and gave me a half-smile and busied herself with her salad.

When the waitress was gone, Allison leaned over the table said, "So he's a bad werewolf?"

"A bad doggy?"

She giggled. "Yes."

"You could say that," I said.

In fact, Nancy had said more than that. Apparently, her ex-boyfriend did more than transform each full moon. He killed, too.

"Killed, how?" she asked, reading my thoughts.

"In a cabin in the woods."

"We have woods here?"

"Arrowhead, ding dong," I said.

"Oh, right, and don't be mean."

I sighed, and continued. "Apparently, he...preps for his turnings."

"Preps, how?"

"With bodies."

"Live bodies?"

"Yes."

"But how..."

"Hikers mostly. Kidnapped, drugged, locked up in his cabin's basement. Where he, in turn, locks himself up each full moon."

"And then what?" asked Allison, eyes wide. "Wait, I don't wanna—"

"He feasts on them, of course."

"...know," she finished, turning a little green.

The waitress came by with our bill. I thought paying was the least I could do, since Allison suddenly looked traumatized. Hearing about a werewolf exploring his true nature—his powerful nature—and feasting on weakling humans, didn't quite haunt me the same way it did Allison. I also knew this was the demon inside me. Or, rather, her influence on me. Or was it? These days, I wasn't quite sure. This should have concerned me more than it did.

"Well, it concerns me, Sam," she said. "And thanks for lunch. I think."

"Oh, cheer up," I said.

"You sound oddly perky for someone who just told me that a local werewolf has a kill room up in Arrowhead."

"Not perky...intrigued."

"Okay, that might be even worse. And he confessed to all of this while asleep?"

"Apparently so."

"What are you going to do next?"

I looked at the time on my cell. "Meet with Kingsley. You know, my *first* choice." I winked as we stood.

"I hate you, Samantha Moon."

"No, you don't."

"You're right, I don't...but don't be surprised if you push me away someday into the arms of another bestie."

"One can hope," I said, and nudged her with my elbow as we left the café.

The red-haired girl watched me the whole way.

6.

I was in Kingsley's office, waiting.

These days, Kingsley employs male receptionists and secretaries. I might have had something to do with that. Kingsley, a known playboy, didn't need the temptation. Did I trust him these days? Mostly. Did he need a blond bimbo leaning over his desk with her cleavage showing, looking to move up in the world of paralegals? Hell, no.

I knew he loved me, and I seriously doubted he would do anything to screw this up again. Then again...

"Once a cheater, always a cheater," or so my sister liked to tell me.

Except I knew that Kingsley was looking for something more, something real, and something with another immortal. Truth was, my own choices were quite limited, since I tended to turn mortals into love slaves. Not a bad idea in theory, but in practice, it was miserable. Try getting through your day when another is literally waiting on you hand and foot, and mostly underfoot.

Yesss, came a voice deep within me.

Of course, *she* would approve. For all I knew, she was instrumental in creating the love slave bond-thing. Which made sense, since she wanted to enslave me, too. To control me completely and totally.

I continued walking through Kingsley's spacious office. The hairy oaf was still into his moons. Everywhere I looked was another full moon. In fact, he had some new additions since the last time I'd been here. The moon globe was new, as was the moon mouse pad and, yes, there was an actual moon rock fragment sitting inside a glass case next to his wet bar. A single spotlight shone down on the rock, which itself was encased in a domed glass. How the man had acquired it, I didn't know. Could you buy moon rocks on eBay?

I was leaning down, peering at it closely, when I heard the door whisper open, and felt a presence enter the room. A very big presence. "It's from the Apollo 14 mission," said a deep voice from behind me, so deep that I seemingly felt it in my own chest. Hell, if I listened close enough, I would have probably heard the glass case rattle. "It's also highly illegal to own it."

"I should turn you in, counselor," I said, turning.

I hadn't even made a complete turn when the big guy pounced, faster than he had any right to pounce, defying physics and, no doubt, straining his expensive suit to the limit. He was on me before I knew it, turning me all the way around, his mouth covering mine, his hair hanging down all over me. To say that he smothered me would be an understatement. To say that I didn't love it would be a lie.

It took all my willpower to push him off me, which I did. He didn't go willingly.

"Down boy," I said, using nearly all my strength to pry the big lug nut off me.

He pushed back his mane of thick hair. He propped a hand on the wall above me and leaned down. I could have been in the shadow of a giant sequoia. "To what do I owe this unexpected visit?"

I stepped under his arm, ducking, although I didn't need to duck. I adjusted my shirt and hair, both of which had been thoroughly groped and mauled and pulled by his giant man-hands.

"I had the strong need to be felt up," I said.

"Really?" He moved toward me again, clearly moved by my romantic words.

"No, ding-a-ling." I held him back at arm's length. The thing about dating a known playboy and an alpha male is, well, they have a high testosterone level, and they know how to get what they want. And they're used to getting what they want. The trick is to make them earn it. Work for it. Beg for it.

But now, of course, wasn't the time or place for any of that, as much as I liked to see Kingsley beg. I asked, "Do you know a man named Gunther Kessler?"

He blinked...and seemed to deflate a little, which wasn't a bad thing, under the circumstances. Kingsley all hopped-up on testosterone and adrenaline tended not to be the best conversationalist.

He sighed and crossed his arms and sat on the corner of his oversized desk. I might have thought he was compensating with such a huge desk...but I knew better. The man wasn't compensating. He was just huge, and growing steadily at the same time. Yes, the big oaf was only getting oafier as the years went on. How big he would eventually get remained to be seen.

"No, why?" he asked.

Unlike Allison and most mortals, I didn't have a telepathic link with Kingsley and other immortals. That wasn't quite true. I did have a telepathic link to the Librarian, who was immortal via alchemical means.

Anyway, Kingsley couldn't read my mind, nor I his, which was probably a good thing.

"He's a werewolf," I said. "I think."

Kingsley raised an eyebrow—an eyebrow that was one or two tweezings away from being a unibrow. "I don't know all the werewolves in the area. Some, but not all."

"How many *are* in the area?" I asked.

"A few dozen of us, but this is also Southern

California."

"Werewolf mecca of the universe?" I said.

"No, but a highly populated part of the country, although you will generally find more werewolves up north."

"Where it's cooler," I said.

"We do tend to be on the plus size," he said. "So, what about this guy?" Kingsley crossed his arms over a massive chest.

Did I detect a hint of jealousy?

"He's a killer," I said. "I think."

"What do you mean?"

I told him what I knew about Gunther. About talking in his sleep. About the cabin in the mountains. About the killing room. About the feeding.

Kingsley stared at me while I spoke. In fact, I was fairly certain he didn't blink either.

Just a couple of freaks.

The difference being, of course, his eyes glowed amber. What color mine glowed, I hadn't a clue, since I hadn't seen them in nine years. My sister had told me that my eyes had turned a darkish brown, almost black. They had once been blue. I sighed at that all over again.

When I was finished, Kingsley pushed off the desk and walked over to the wet bar, where he poured himself a finger or two of Crystal Skull vodka, which seemed fitting under the circumstances.

"Some werewolves hunger for fresh blood," he

said. "Or live food."

"You don't," I said, and it was a memory I would rather forget. The one time Kingsley had escaped his own "safe room," which was deep under his estate home, he had gone straight to a local cemetery...and dug up a freshly buried body. That he had consumed it was something that should have been a dealbreaker for me. Luckily, Kingsley didn't have much control over himself when he was in his changeling state.

Still...so gross. *And I kiss that mouth.*

"No, Sam. I don't hunger for fresh blood. But many do. In fact, we're very nearly divided down the middle."

"Half prefer corpses, half prefer the living."

He winced a little. "Right."

We both knew what the wince meant...and we both let it go. I doubted Kingsley was proud of his actions. Then again, he had very little control of his actions, either, although he had ended up in my hotel room...and had restrained himself from attacking me. *Somehow.*

I said, "Well, there's a chance he's killed many."

"I don't doubt it, Sam. Not all werewolves are responsible, Sam. Nor are all vampires. Some kill. Some love to kill. But, like you and me, many of us take precautions against our true natures."

My precaution was feeding regularly from Allison—and, if desperate enough, from the packs of cow and pig blood in my refrigerator in the garage. Kingsley had a holding cell beneath his house. A safe room.

I said, "Well, he's taking precautions, too. Except he's locking up hikers with him."

Food, although I couldn't bring myself to say it.

The entity within me was enjoying this conversation very much. I felt her rise up through my consciousness so that she wouldn't miss a word. *Crazy bitch.*

"Some people are killers before they turn, Sam," said Kingsley. "And some of us give in to the darkness within us."

"And feed the demons within us," I said.

"Right. It takes willpower and fortitude to stay true to ourselves."

"Tell me about it," I said, and sighed.

As he drank, I considered having a finger or two of vodka myself, but I had to pick up the kids soon, and, although alcohol had no effect on me, it wouldn't be a good thing picking up the kids with vodka breath. The principal already didn't like me as it was.

Instead, I folded my arms over my own chest and drummed my pointed fingernails along my upper arm. "He's going to have to be stopped."

"I agree," said Kingsley. "Let me ask around, see what I can find out on the guy."

"Thank you."

"And Sam?"

"Yes?"

He sighed loudly. "Please be careful."

I stood on my tippy-toes and ruffled his thick mane of hair...and planted a big kiss on his thick lips.

"Always," I said, and left.

7.

It was late.

Although I now existed nicely in the sun, I had gotten used to my late-night hours. My vampire hours. Turns out, working late and private investigations sort of go hand-in-hand. Plus, the night time just...suited me. I felt comfortable under the cloak of darkness...and exposed and vulnerable in daylight. After all, I was just a vigorous hand-washing away from losing my precious amethyst ring down, say, a sink drain, and then where would I be? Back to working the night shift, permanently. And shrieking in the light of day like the pathetic monster I am.

Now, making a mental note to use minimum amounts of soap—I relaxed in the back seat of my minivan and kept a watchful eye on Gunther Kessler's two-story home.

The lights had been out when I pulled up thirty minutes ago. There was a Dodge Charger parked out front. The home was a turn-of-the-century wooden deal, with a wraparound porch and lots of shutters. A half-dozen wide cement stairs led up to the front door. Very typical for Old Town Orange, an area I loved.

It was past midnight and the kids were asleep. These days, I often left them alone. Tammy was thirteen and Anthony was eleven going on twenty. Meaning, he didn't look anything like your typical eleven-year-old. After my son had lost his own guardian angel—long story—Ishmael, my ex-guardian angel, had imbued Anthony with all sorts of angelic powers, some of which had caused my boy to grow a bit taller than your average eleven-year-old. And to become far stronger than your average eleven-year-old, too. Hell, far stronger than even your average adult male.

Anyway, now my son acted as his own guardian angel, meaning, he could take care of himself and then some.

Of course, I'm pretty sure Ishmael did all of this to get on my good side, to sort of make up for his negligence in protecting me, back when I was first turned nine years ago.

Truth was, his gesture to help my son did go far. I appreciated it. My life was weird enough without having to worry that my son no longer had his guardian angel.

Now, he didn't need a guardian angel. Now, my son was a hell of a force to be reckoned with.

And he was only eleven.

Sweet mama.

Now, I was on a quiet street in downtown Orange, near the offices of a private investigator friend of mine, Mercedes Cruz. Mercedes, or Mercy, was a different kind of strange altogether. She was, I was certain, a witch. Of course, she and I didn't discuss such matters. Nor did we discuss that I was a vampire, although I always suspected she knew. Witches are like that. What we did discuss was our kids, our work, our mutual friends, all while eyeing each other suspiciously. Anyway, I knew she was doing good work here in Orange, protecting the legal—and illegal—immigrants from those who would take advantage of them. Like I said, good work.

Whether she knew of any local werewolves or not, I didn't know.

Then again, I wasn't certain Gunther was a werewolf. I had only the word of my dead ex-husband's mistress. And even then, he'd only been talking in his sleep.

"What am I doing here?" I said.

Easy. Nancy had caught me in a lull. No pending cases, and certainly no paying cases. And, no, she hadn't offered to pay me either. Still, try as I might to hate her, I just couldn't. Truth, with Danny now dead, most of my anger had died, too.

As she'd said, if it hadn't been her, it would have been another girl at Danny's strip club.

I know how to pick 'em.

Earlier, I had run Gunther Kessler's name through my various databases. Outside of his downtown Orange home, there was nothing to suggest he even owned a home in Arrowhead, where Nancy claimed he had a "killing room." A place where he turned from human to werewolf on each full moon. And where, apparently, he feasted on the living.

I drummed my pointed fingernails on my steering wheel.

The demoness within me was highly interested in this line of thinking. I could feel her following along, mostly approving of what she was hearing. She enjoyed death and destruction. She enjoyed feasting on the weak. She knew that fear made people less powerful, and her more powerful.

Yesss, came the single word.

For the most part, I'd been able to contain her in a small section of my mind, but she often figured a way out, slipping back into my consciousness like smoke under a doorway. These days, I didn't mind when she slipped through. Other than being a psychopath hell-bent on taking over the world, I found her company...less and less annoying.

Shaking my head over the insanity of it all, I continued to watch Gunther Kessler's home, all the way up through the morning.

Interestingly, not one but two cars sporting big,

furry mustaches on their grills drove past me on the street. One was odd enough...but two?

I nearly Googled "cars with furry mustaches" when Gunther's front door opened and he stepped outside. I knew it was him because Nancy had emailed me pictures of him. Not to mention I had done a Google search on him and found his Facebook page. Yes, even werewolves had Facebook pages.

If he was a werewolf.

Anyway, he was dressed in a suit and tie, with his long hair gleaming wet. A medium-sized man, he headed straight to his Dodge Charger parked in the driveway. He clicked it open, got in, and backed out.

When he was halfway down the street, I forgot about the cars with mustaches and eased away from the curb to follow him.

***

I didn't follow him for long.

After a brief stop at a Starbucks—where I longed to follow him inside but somehow restrained myself—he soon pulled into the parking lot of American Title in Orange, off Main Street, about a mile away from where Kingsley worked. *Here be monsters.*

I stopped along a curb and watched him park near the front of the building. Assigned parking, surely. He got out, went around to his trunk and removed his laptop bag. Then he headed through some smoky glass doors, through which he disappeared.

Other than the longish hair, he didn't look like much of a werewolf. Kingsley, I could believe. This guy? I didn't know.

But I would find out.

I pulled away from the curb and hit up the very same Starbucks frequented by Gunther earlier, and ordered myself a venti mocha with extra mocha and extra whipped cream. I also ordered a bagel with extra cream cheese. Go big, or go home, as Anthony would say.

Long ago, I had arranged for a neighbor to take my kids to school, since, back then, I tended to be comatose in the morning. I saw no need to change the schedule. After all, during cases like this one, I might find myself working all night and well into the morning.

Or at Starbucks.

8.

We were in the kitchen, us girls.

My sister, Mary Lou, myself and my daughter. It was later that same day, Thursday, which also happened to be our *Vampire Diaries* night. That's right, as if my life wasn't crazy enough, I also watched fictional vampires on TV...and loved every minute of it.

Not only did I love the show, I studied it. I seriously think that someone on staff was a vampire. They get so much right. Not everything, granted, but enough that I have learned much, well, about myself.

Now we were making spaghetti with spicy sausages, which happened to be Anthony's favorite, too. On Thursdays, he mostly made himself scarce, although I often caught him keeping an eye on the TV. I think he was a closet *Diaries* fan, although he wouldn't admit it. Had the show been called something like *The Vampire Scrolls*, he would have been all over it. *Boys.*

Now the three of us girls were in my kitchen, each with a job to do, although Tammy's job seemed to devolve into leaning against the counter and drinking her grape juice, while watching us with a smirk on her face. Mary Lou and I were drinking wine from goblets. Would a vampire drink wine from anything less?

"Oh, brother," said Tammy, rolling her eyes. She sipped some more of her drink.

"Oh, brother what?" I asked. I was chopping cucumbers for the salad. Mary Lou had been in the middle of telling me another work story. There was a slight chance I might have zoned out. Slight.

"I'm pretty sure not *all* vampires drink from goblets, Mom. And since when did you start calling yourself a *vampire*, anyway? I thought you hated that word."

I stopped chopping and looked at my daughter. She knew better than to read my mind when her aunt was around. Or read my mind, period. We had talked about it. Ad nauseam.

"Are you freakin' kidding me?" said Mary Lou, turning on me.

"Mary Lou..." I began.

"No, Sam. It's bad enough that you and Allison go around reading each other's minds, but now you and your daughter, too?"

I set my knife down and glared at my daughter. *You're in trouble, Missy,* I thought. Then to Mary Lou, I said, "It's not like that..."

"Oh, and what's it not like, Sam? Not to mention I'm pretty darn certain that you just, you know, *thought* something to your daughter."

"Yes, but—"

"But what? I thought you couldn't read family members' minds, Sam."

"I can't, but—"

"I thought we had an agreement, Samantha. No more leaving me out."

I took hold of her shoulders before she could work herself into a full-fledged tizzy. Behind me, Tammy giggled. I would deal with her later. "I can't read your mind, Louie. And I can't read my daughter's mind, either. But she can read mine. And she can read yours. Unless you learn how to block her out."

"I can even read Kingsley's," said Tammy. "He doesn't know it, but I can."

I hadn't thought of that before. My daughter, being the super mind reader that she was, could potentially read *anyone's* mind, mortal or immortal.

"Of course, Mommy."

We'll, talk about this later, young lady, I thought.

Meanwhile, Mary Lou didn't like being held in place by me, but tough shit. She had started this little tirade and I wasn't letting her go until she calmed down. Luckily, my words were finally sinking in.

"Tammy can read my mind?"

"Yes," I said.

Mary Lou looked from me to my daughter. Then, for some damn reason, my goofball sister actually smiled. "Really?"

"Yes, really," I said. "And this makes you happy, why?"

"Because I don't feel left out now! I feel, you know, like part of the gang."

"Of course you're part of the gang, Mary Lou, and I think you've had enough wine for tonight."

"But I just got started..."

"You've had a rough day," I said, and began steering her out of the kitchen and into the living room. "Just sit down and relax. We'll take it from here."

She called back over her shoulder. "What am I thinking now, Tammy?"

"Aunt Louie!" giggled Tammy.

I didn't have to be a mind reader to know where this was going. "Let me guess," I said, steering her toward the couch. "Damon."

They both giggled as I deposited my sister in front of the TV. Once back in the kitchen, I again didn't need to be a mind reader to know that my daughter was acting a little strange. I needed only to be a mother. I snatched her "grape juice" out of her hand and sniffed it.

Uh-oh.

9.

It was after *The Vampire Diaries*.

Truth was, I didn't much enjoy the show this week. Sure, Damon looked sexy. Even Stefan had his moments. The others in the cast were electrifying and gory and funny. The plotline was convoluted but ingenious, and all in all, a great addition to the series.

Except, of course, I was having trouble concentrating on it.

Now with my sister mostly sober and gone home, and still giddy that she wasn't being left out of the cool group, I sat with my daughter in her bedroom.

Anthony had gone home with my sister, as well. I didn't want him to overhear us. Turned out, his hearing was getting better and better, too. Too good for my comfort. The kid was turning into Captain America.

Or Captain Skidmarks.

"That's funny, Mom."

"Don't try to get on my good side," I said. "And yes, that was kind of funny."

She giggled. I was fairly certain the alcohol hadn't worn off yet. It had, after all, only been an hour or so. "What have I told you about reading my thoughts?"

"I'm not supposed to. But sometimes, I can't help it."

I knew the feeling. I said, "I know you can't help it, honey. And sometimes, I can't help it either. But I want you to do your best to not listen in on adult conversations."

"I'm sorry."

"And don't listen in on your brother's thoughts, either."

"Gross. I learned my lesson about him, Mommy. Do you know that sometimes all he thinks about, for like ten straight minutes, is boobies?"

My son, of course, was eleven going on an apparently early puberty. I said, "I could have gone my whole life without knowing that."

"Well, now we both know it," and she giggled some more and, despite myself, I giggled, too. "Why do boys like boobies so much, Mommy?"

I opened my mouth to answer. "Honestly? I haven't the faintest idea."

She found that funny, too, and laughed harder...until she saw the serious look on my face.

"Uh-oh," she said.

"Uh-oh is right, young lady."

"You're mad, aren't you?"

"Says the girl who can read my mind."

"What does that mean?"

"It means you know darn well that I'm mad."

"It was just a little wine," she said. "And it was so good. No wonder you and Auntie love it so much!"

Uh-oh.

"Honey, wine is for adults. You know that."

"Well, I'm thirteen. I'm a teenager. I'm in middle school. Half the kids in my school drink beer."

"Half?"

"Well, some. And Angie Harmon's mom lets her drink at home, on special occasions."

I rubbed my face. I might have moaned.

"And I figured tonight was a special occasion!"

Now, I was massaging my temples.

"And it's not like I'm out drinking with friends on some street corner."

Now I definitely moaned.

"I drank responsibly, Mom."

I hugged my knees and started rocking on her bed. Rocking and moaning and wishing my sweet, innocent little girl wasn't saying words like "drinking responsibly."

"It's not that bad, Mom. Just a little wine.

Sheesh, get over it—"

That's when I'd had enough. I quit playing the victim and took in a lot of unnecessary air, mostly to clear my mind and to calm myself down, and said, "I will not get over it, young lady. I will get right on top of it. In fact, I will get right inside it."

"Gross."

"If I *ever* see or hear of you drinking again, you are going to be in a lot of trouble."

"I'm a teenager—"

"You are thirteen and far too young to be drinking."

"But Angie and almost everyone at school—"

"I don't care about Angie and almost everyone at your school. I care about you. My daughter. Who's far too young to handle alcohol—"

"But I drank responsibly!"

"If I hear you say, 'I drank responsibly' again, I'm going to homeschool you for the rest of your life."

"You can't do that."

"I can do anything I want."

"Then I will tell everyone you're a vampire! And a killer!"

My mouth fell open. It stayed open for a long, long time.

"I'm sorry, Mommy. I would never do that. Ever."

"You think I'm a killer?" I finally asked.

Tammy looked away, tears forming in the corners of her eyes. "I...I don't know, Mommy."

"You've seen me kill," I thought. "In my memory."

"Yes. You've done it a few times."

"You shouldn't be in there, baby. Ever."

She nodded, which shook free the tears.

I said, "Mommy had to...do what she had to do."

She kept on shaking her head.

"Baby, I'm sorry you had to see that."

"It's okay, Mommy. They were bad men."

I mentally ran through the horrors of the past few years. *Jesus*, I thought.

I took in some air. "You need to stay out of Mommy's thoughts, baby. Okay?"

"Okay."

"Do you promise?"

"I'll try." She paused, and what she said next had me laughing harder than it should have. "Now do you see why I was driven to drink?"

When I was done laughing into my hands, tears streaming down my cheeks—and I wasn't entirely sure if some of those tears weren't real tears—I grabbed her feet and proceeded to tickle them until she promised to never drink again.

Ever.

10.

The Occult Reading Room wasn't empty.

A man was doing just that: reading in a chair in the far corner, very near the darkest, creepiest of the books. The books that seemed to possess a dark intelligence. The books that seemed, in fact, to be alive.

I heard their whisperings now as the man read. The whisperings sounded more excited than usual. In fact, they hardly seemed to notice me at all. They were, in fact, focused on the man reading.

"You hear them, too, right? The books?" I asked the Librarian, whose real name was Archibald Maximus. He was Max to me sometimes. Or even Archie. Other than my daughter, Max was the only other entity alive who seemed capable of reading my thoughts. He also seemed to have all the answers, which is why I came around. That he was easy on the eyes had nothing to do with it at all. I swear.

"Yes, Sam. I hear them. In fact, I hear all of them."

"All of them?"

"They each speak, Sam. Some louder than others."

"But...how?"

He looked at me, then at a book stacked on a nearby counter, and said, "As you know, these aren't your average books. These books have been imbued with intent, some even written in blood."

"So, you're saying they're...haunted?"

"Not quite, Sam. But energy is attracted to them. Sometimes dark energy, but usually, just an *aspect* of that energy."

"Not the entire entity."

"Right, Sam. Just like not all of you is contained within your physical vessel."

"An aspect of me?"

"An idea of you, Sam. Your soul. Your real soul lies in the energetic world, observing all of this with interest."

"So, who am I, then?"

"Think of yourself as a representative of who you really are."

"Are you trying to hurt my brain?"

He laughed. "Some of this is not easy to understand. Much of it was never really meant to be understood, except by those who seek answers or..."

"By those of us who are forced to find answers."

"Yes, Sam. For most of the world, the search for spiritual truth is a personal journey of their choosing. For you, your spiritual journey was thrust on you."

"And by thrust," I said, "you mean forced upon me, when I was attacked and turned into what I am now."

"Your attack has left you seeking bigger answers, and has exposed you to the world of spirit. And often, the underbelly of the world of spirit. For there is darkness out there, Sam. Great darkness. Powerful darkness, as you are well aware."

"I *am* the darkness," I said.

He shook his head. "They might have made a very, very big mistake coming after you, Sam. They might have unleashed their own undoing."

"I'm just a mom..."

"With a powerful bloodline."

"Lucky me," I said.

"Perhaps unlucky for them. They have taken a chance by making you one of their own."

"Because they need me..."

"Yes, Sam. But the person they most need...is the very person who can destroy them."

"You do realize that I'll be picking up my kids in thirty minutes, right? I won't be destroying anyone anytime soon."

He laughed. "Let's consider it a process."

"Fine," I said. "Back to the books. Are you

saying they're possessed?"

"In a way, yes."

"Well, they're possessed enough to beckon me."

"I imagine they do, Sam."

"Why?"

"Because the energy within some of them recognize the thing that is within you."

"That thing being your mother," I corrected.

"*Was* my mother," he said. "She hasn't been my mother for a very long time."

I thought I detected a note.

"There is no note, Sam."

I wasn't so sure about that. I said, "Do you miss her?"

"It's hard to miss a monster."

Another note, whether he wanted to admit it or not. "Do you still love her?"

"Fine," he said. "Yes, I love the memory of her, back when I was young, back when there was some semblance of good within her. Back before she was lured..."

"Don't say it..."

"To the dark side."

"You said it," I said, and grinned.

He did, too, then sighed heavily. "Melodramatic, I know. But true. She was different back in the day. She was a real mother."

"What turned her?"

"That's a story best told another day, Sam."

"Fine," I said. "But I want to know. After all, your mother is very much a part of me now."

He looked at me long and hard. "I know."

"She wants me to let her out. She wants to talk to you. She wants to apologize for all that she's done—"

"You can't let her out, Sam. Ever. Remember that. The moment she gets out, you will no longer be able to control her. *Ever.*"

"What...what do you mean?" I asked, gasping slightly. His mother's presence was strong in me, stronger than I had ever felt before. Pulsing at my temples. My head literally felt like it might explode.

"Think of it like a neural pathway. Once established, she will always be able to access it again and again."

I took a deep breath, and, using all my willpower, pushed her back down, back into the mental box I envisioned her trapped inside. I even threw up another mental wall or two, sealing her in.

Once done, I opened my eyes, blinking hard. Even the muted light within the Occult Reading Room seemed too bright. I shied from it, turning my head. As I did so, I noticed the man who had been reading was gone. I blinked, sure I was seeing things...but there was no one there.

"You okay, Sam?"

"Your mom's a bitch."

"Tell me about it."

"She...she almost got out," I said. "I almost let her, just to release the pressure."

He nodded and released my hand. "Maybe it was a bad idea bringing her around me."

I didn't know what to say to that, but I did push back my black hair. My forehead was sweating. My temples still throbbed.

"You're right, of course," he said after a moment. "I'm not just keeping an eye on her."

I waited. My head still hurt, reminding me what a headache felt like, since I hadn't had one in nearly nine years.

"She's pivotal for stopping all of this," said Maximus.

"All of what?"

"The infusion of dark masters into our world."

"In the form of vampires and werewolves," I said.

"Yes," he said. "And others."

"What others?"

"There's more under the sun, or moon, than just vampires and werewolves, Sam. The dark masters take many forms."

"Like the soul-jumping demon," I said, remembering my memorable vacation on a small island in the Pacific Northwest.

"Right," he said. "But that's not important now."

"Sure," I said, still rubbing my head, and looking over at the now-empty reading chair. "Why worry about all sorts of monsters roaming our streets?"

"There are not as many as you might think, Sam."

"Seems that way."

"As they say, like attracts like. The dark masters gravitate toward each other."

"Sounds like a party," I said.

"A dead man's party."

"Good one, Max. So, what's this about your mother being pivotal to stopping all this craziness?"

"She and one other," said the Librarian.

"Dracula," I said, remembering our conversation from last year. Dracula, who was the first vampire.

The Librarian nodded. "Indeed. The son of the dragon."

I knew my history, limited as it was. *Dracul*, of course, meant House of the Dragon. Dracula meant, in turn, son of the dragon.

"Very good, Sam," he said, picking up my thoughts. "There's something I haven't told you yet."

"That doesn't sound promising," I said.

He pressed his lips together and looked at me, then looked away, then looked at me again.

And then it hit me. "Oh, no," I said.

"Oh yes," he said.

"You're not going to tell me..."

He nodded. "They were in love, Sam. At least, I think it was love. For all I know, it could have been a convenient bonding. A convenient union of dark masters."

"Wait, are you telling me..."

"Yes, Sam. The entity that's within Dracula is and forever will be, in love with my mother."

"Ah, shit," I said.

"Ah, shit, is right."

11.

I met Sheriff Stanley at a coffee shop in a small mountain town called Crestline, gateway into the San Bernardino Mountains.

The coffee shop had probably been any number of shops over its lifetime. The building was old and nestled under a Mexican restaurant that sported, I noted on a chalkboard near the wooden stairs leading up to it, wine-a-ritas.

"First off," I said to the sheriff, after he shook my hand and I sat opposite him, "what's a wine-a-rita?"

"A margarita made with wine," he said. Sheriff Stanley was a young guy who sported an old-school mustache.

I understood quickly enough. "They lost their

liquor license."

"Hard liquor."

"Are the wine-a-ritas any good?"

"I tried it once."

"And?"

"I think I vomited a little in the back of my mouth. But then," he shrugged and rubbed his mustache, "I dunno, they kind of grow on you. I guess they're not the worst thing in the world. Still, kinda makes my stomach turn a little just thinking about them."

"Let me get you a coffee," I said.

"Black," he said. "Blacker than black."

"Says the guy who ordered a wine-a-rita."

"I don't know you well enough for you to bust my chops."

I shrugged. "Never stopped me before."

I slid out of the booth and ordered our coffees.

***

Sweet nectar of the gods, I thought.

The gift of coffee might have been the greatest gift that Maximus—and his rings—could have given me. After eight years of not having the stuff, now, I couldn't get enough of it, especially since the caffeine didn't have any effect. Nor did alcohol. My body neutralized both equally.

Luckily, my addiction for coffee went beyond the caffeine high. It was the taste. The aroma. The experience. Coffee made me feel human. And humanity is what I needed most if I wanted to keep the thing inside me at bay.

"Should I, uh, leave you alone with your coffee?" asked Sheriff Stanley.

"Now, who's busting whose balls?"

"Hey, I'm not the one moaning and groaning over my coffee."

"You would," I said, "if you had the day I had."

"Look, Miss—"

"Ms."

"What the fuck is the difference?"

"*Miss* implies a woman who's never been married. *Ms.* is an indefinite title for a woman whose marital status is unknown."

"Well, you ain't wearing a wedding ring. Just those other rings."

I set the coffee mug down. "*Ms.* is also an appropriate title for a divorcee, which I happen to be."

He wanted to say something smart-alecky, or rude, or show me how tough he was since he now regretted owning up to drinking the wine-a-rita. He opened his mouth and I was prepared for more bluster. After all, I was used to such bluster, having spent much of my professional life working in the male-dominated field of law enforcement. Instead, he closed it again and sort of rebooted.

"Sorry about the divorced part," he said. "I'm going through that right now. It really sucks."

"I'm sorry to hear that," I said.

He nodded, sighed.

"Any kids involved?"

He shook his head. "Elise and I were talking about having kids, until..."

"Until what?"

"Never mind," he said. "I don't know you well enough to burden you."

I nodded and dipped into his mind and—right there at the forefront of his thoughts—I saw him opening the door to his bedroom and seeing his wife with another man. Then the scene looped again. And again.

"She cheated on you," I said.

Sheriff Stanley was a young guy, maybe thirty-two. I caught a glimpse of something else in his thoughts. Something he had dreamed about often. I saw three kids running. I saw him playing with them, a sort of game of hide-and-seek. Two girls and a boy. Now, he was rolling in the grass with them. A golden retriever bounded between them, licking indiscriminately. Someone had seen one too many episodes of *Full House*. Kids were fun, but maybe not that fun. Scratch that. Anthony was a hoot. And so was Tammy, in her way. It's just that...well, it's just that it's not all fun and games.

Anyway, I could have laughed at his innocent, almost naïve approach to having a family. In fact, I might have if I didn't feel his overwhelming sense of loss. He wanted a family, and he had thought it would be with the woman he'd caught cheating.

He nodded. "That obvious?"

I held his gaze and felt his loss and heard him

crying inside. He didn't know I could hear the sobs that echoed through his memories. "Lucky guess," I said softly, and reached out and patted his hand.

His aura sort of reached out to me. That man needed a hug in a bad way, but then, it recoiled and he pulled back his hand. "I don't really wanna talk about it, you know?"

"I know," I said.

After a moment, he said, "Did your old man cheat on you, too?"

"He did," I said.

"Pretty shitty thing to do to someone who loves you, huh?"

"About as shitty as it gets," I said. That, and trying to kill them, too, which was what Danny had tried to do in the end, with the help of a vampire named Hanner.

I saw something else in his mind. I saw his wife apologizing over and over. I saw her weeping, begging. I saw her phone calls and the texts. Her appearing at his work, at the apartment he had moved into.

"Who was the guy?" I asked.

"Her old boyfriend. A friend of mine, too. We go back to high school, all of us."

"Are they together now?"

"No," he said quickly, and looked very uncomfortable talking to me. "Elise said it was a mistake."

Relax, I thought.

He nodded and took a deep breath, cracked his

neck, and sank a little deeper into his seat. We could have been two friends lounging on a couch, playing X-Box in our basketball shorts.

Not that relaxed, I thought.

He nodded and sat up a little, unaware that I was prompting him with my suggestions.

"Why did she do it?" I asked, and added telepathically: *It's okay to talk to me, I'm a friend.*

He looked at me, cocked his head slightly, nodded. He really didn't want to talk about it. In fact, I was fairly certain, outside of a few close guy friends and family, he hadn't talk about it at all.

"We were fighting. I left in a huff. I said something stupid."

"How stupid?"

"I told her I should never have married her. That it was a mistake, and that I might go look up an old girlfriend."

"That's a whole lot of stupid in a row," I said.

"Tell me about it," he said. "So then, Elise calls her ex-boyfriend."

"And the rest is history," I said.

He nodded.

"And now, you won't forgive her?" I asked.

"Did you forgive your old man?"

I shook my head. "He didn't give me a chance. He moved on. But I have forgiven someone else...and it's not easy."

"My mom says once a cheater, always a cheater."

"Maybe," I said. "Or maybe not. No one knows

the future. People make mistakes. People learn from their mistakes."

He shrugged, still uncomfortable despite my mental prompting. As we sat there, and as I considered what to say to him, if anything, three entities materialized in the booth behind him. Small entities, although they were too fuzzy to make out any real details.

Kids, I realized. Unborn kids. Which was a first to me. I had seen the spirits of the departed...but never the not-yet-born. Until now.

"You wanted to build a family with her."

"Yes."

"Her and only her," I said.

"Elise was my everything," he said. "I screwed it all up. And she sure as hell didn't help."

Now the smallish spirits slipped over the booth and pushed up next to him. One sat on his lap, except he didn't know it, of course. I watched in amazement as another crawled up onto his shoulder and the third, the girl, curled under his arm. He shivered.

"Do you still love her?" I asked after a moment.

"Yeah," he said. He looked away, fighting the tears, jaw quivering. "I don't know why I'm telling you all of this."

"Maybe I'm easy to talk to."

"Maybe."

It's okay to cry, I told him.

And he did now, but not very hard. It wouldn't be very becoming for the town sheriff to weep loudly at the little coffee shop. But the tears flowed anyway, silently; he didn't bother to wipe them away.

"Yeah, I love her, but I can't..." He cried a little harder now, and this time, he did reach up to wipe his cheeks and eyes. "I can't forgive her, Ms. Moon. I can't. I don't know how to. I just don't...know how..."

One or two people looked over at us. I telepathically told those one or two people to mind their own business. They did, turning their backs to us.

I considered what to do, even as the spirits swarmed around the grief-stricken man. *Their future father.* One even tried to wipe the tears from his face, and I knew what I had to do.

***

Give me your hands, I told him.

He blinked rapidly, eyelashes beaded with tears, then held out both of his hands. Thick, calloused hands.

Look at me. Good. Now, can you hear me?
"Yes."
Speak to me only in your mind.
Like this?
Yes. Good.

I slipped deeper into his consciousness, and pushed through the pain and confusion and loss and hurt, deeper than I had any right to be.

There, buried under the jealousy and grief was something bright and glowing and spinning slightly. I knew what this was from my experience with Russell, my boyfriend from two years ago, the man who had inadvertently become my love slave. Of course, finding Russell's higher self or soul had been a lot harder, for it had been buried deep, deep beneath the curse that was, well, me.

Sheriff Stanley was only a few layers down, although his grief was real and, if left unchecked, it would be lifelong. Grief like this would, I assumed, give him issues for the rest of his life, from distrust of other women to never feeling secure and loved and worthy.

And so, I spoke to him directly, to this higher aspect of himself. I told him to find the courage to let it all go, to find the courage to forgive her and to accept the responsibility of his own actions. I reminded him that he had a family to build with her, and with my words, I flamed his love for her back to life. The love was real, and it was deep, and it was easy to flame to life.

Most important, I told him to forget he ever met me. When I was done, when I slipped back out of his mind and found myself sitting across from him again, I released his hands and sat back.

He blinked, blinked again, then said, "I have to go."

"Figured you did," I said, and grinned.

He stopped as he was getting out of the booth. "Wait, who are you?"

I waved him away. "I'm not really here, remember?"

"Oh, right."

And then, he was gone, dashing through the coffee shop to, I assumed, his wife. The three staticy, small entities trailed after him. They were holding hands and skipping.

12.

I was at the park ranger station just outside Arrowhead.

This time, I made it a point to get to the point. My last meeting had gone precisely nowhere, although I might have helped to salvage a relation-ship. And helped to build a family.

Both of which, I knew, pissed off the demoness within me, which was exactly why I had done it. Well, *one* of the reasons. What can I say? I happen to be a romantic at heart.

Ranger Ted sat behind a dented, metallic desk. A coffee mug was warming in an electric coaster that might have been the coolest thing I'd ever seen. Ranger Ted was graying and thin and didn't look very intimidating. Then again, I didn't think his job required him to look very intimidating. I think I could have taken him, vampire or not. The aggressive, competitive side of me was relatively new. I suspected it was *her* bleeding into my personality.

Oh, joy.

At the moment, Ranger Ted was looking through a thick blue folder, which was sub-divided further with little plastic tabs. When he was done flipping through the folder, he looked up at me.

"Nineteen missing," he said, "since 2010. And twelve missing from 2000 to 2010."

"So, nineteen in the last four years," I said. "And twelve in the ten prior to that."

He frowned, not liking the sound of that. "Yup."

"It went from just over one a year to almost five a year."

He nodded and looked pained. "Troubling as hell, I know."

"Any theories?"

He blew some air out, then shrugged. "The mountains are as popular as ever. More hikers means more disappearances."

"Quadruple the hikers?"

"I thought you said five times," he said.

"Caught me," I said. "I couldn't think of the word for increasing fivefold."

"Quintuple," he said.

"Yeah," I said. "That word."

The ranger almost grinned. In fact, he might

have if the missing hiker stats weren't still depressing him. "I'm not sure how I know it, myself. I guess there are benefits to getting old. You come across enough shit over the years, and some of it even manages to stick."

I nodded and felt a sudden surge of relief. Relief knowing that I would never age, never wrinkle, never grow old. Ideally, my memory stayed as sharp as ever, even while I accumulated more and more knowledge. Not a bad deal.

I said, "Are the disappearances centralized anywhere on the mountain?"

"Well, the San Bernardinos are a chain of a dozen mountains. But I would say the bulk of the disappearances are along the popular hiking trails near Arrowhead."

"Who oversees the searches?"

"The San Bernardino County Sheriff. We provide support and aid."

I nodded. "Have any of these hikers ever been found?"

"'Bout fifteen years ago, we found a college professor who'd gone missing for about three days. Found him in a cave, half dehydrated."

"But none in the last fifteen years?"

He shook his head sadly. "I guess we don't have a good track record up here."

I said nothing, and looked again at the topographical map hanging on the wall behind him. It was looking more and more like the missing hikers would never be found.

Especially with a hungry werewolf prowling the woods.

13.

It was nearly dusk.

I hiked alone along a sometimes winding trail, although mostly it meandered through ponderosa pine, cedar, black oak, white oak and dogwoods. I knew this because I had read the posters that lined the park ranger's office. I was a little sketchy on which were the black and white oaks, but other than that, I was fairly proud of myself for picking out the different trees. Granted, none were as big as the pines in the Pacific Northwest, but that was to be expected. This was—according to the chart—a transiticonifer forest, which meant little to me, although it probably got botanists all hot and bothered.

I picked up my pace, although the forest was

getting darker by the minute. Luckily for me, light particles danced and swarmed before my eyes, lighting my way, enough through the darkest of nights...or along a darkening forest trail.

Not quite light particles, I thought, as I picked up my pace even more. *God particles, maybe. Spirit energy, definitely.*

Tree trunks flowed past me. Ferns and smaller bushes swept by. I picked up speed, hitting the trail hard and fast. I could have been on a rollercoaster. Up and down and around tight corners and through mud puddles, up steep slopes and down sharply angled trails that led down into ravines.

Faster, I ran. And faster.

I adjusted my footwork on the fly, supernaturally fast. I should have broken my ankle a hundred times over. Instead, I sidestepped small holes, rocks and tree roots. I pumped my arms and laughed and could have sworn that there were times that my feet didn't even touch the ground. I could have been flying through the forest.

I knew I was grinning from ear to ear as I ran, but I didn't care. No one could see me. I was in the deep, dark woods, which was only getting darker by the minute, although it was becoming more alive to me, alive with flashing light.

Critters scattered in my wake. I surprised two deer on the trail. I moved between them, smelling their musky coats, and hearing them dash off after I was dozens of yards past them. I could have grabbed one. I could have broken its neck. I could have feasted on it. And then what? I would have been covered in deer blood. But it would have been...exciting, invigorating, thrilling.

I pushed past the feeling and continued running. As much as I enjoyed fresh blood, I was enjoying this night run even more.

I found a trail that seemed to lead up, and up I went, higher and higher into the mountains, hurdling logs and boulders and running up a trail I was certain few humans had ever used. A game trail, surely. High above, the quarter moon appeared within a thick stand of Douglas firs.

How far had I run? Two or three miles? Five? Ten? I didn't know, but I knew I was lost as hell...and I didn't care.

Up I went, higher and higher, and, if possible, my speed seemed to only increase.

At one point, I finally did hit a hidden tree root, and I tumbled head over ass, skidding on my face. I got up, spitting out dirt and twigs and laughing. Nothing broken. I wasn't even scratched. I dusted myself off, then started running again, zigzagging up the trail, knowing I was nothing more than a blur to anything watching me, and feeling like I was on the ride of my life.

No wonder I was grinning like a fool, all the way up past the treeline, and over loose rocks and boulders until finally, finally I stood at the top of Old Greyback, the highest peak in the San Bernardinos. At 12,000 feet I finally stopped and looked down upon Southern California far, far below.

I wasn't even out of breath.

I found a cluster of boulders and climbed to the top and sat there and relived my mad dash up the mountain. It had been exhilarating, thrilling—and it had all been possible, courtesy of the demon within.

No, I didn't hate her. She had, in fact, shown me a side of life that few would ever see.

Of course, I knew now that I hadn't been randomly picked, that my bloodline reached all the way to the greatest alchemist of all time, Hermes Trismegistus.

Yes, my bloodline was desirable.

For what, I didn't exactly know, although some of it had to do with helping the dark masters back into this world. Directly. And not through hosts like myself.

Directly and permanently.

I pulled up my legs and wrapped my arms around my knees. There was a hole in my pants. My running shoes were kinda ruined, too, I saw. I didn't think Asics had something like me in mind when they field-tested their products. I flicked a hanging piece of the rubber sole. I needed new shoes anyway.

The wind was strong up here, and infused with a mix of desert and mountain scents. After all, one side of the mountain sloped down into Joshua Tree, one of the more epic of Southern California's deserts, which just so happened to be the name of my favorite U2 album. Yes, I'm showing my age.

Then again, a hundred years from now, with music coming and going and my kids long since dead, I would still have a fondness for 80s' and 90s' alternative rock.

Suddenly depressed, I considered my case. Which was the reason why I'd come up here in the first place.

That something was stalking these woods, I had no doubt. There had been no witnesses, and no evidence of foul play. The bodies had never been found. Something or someone had either consumed them completely, or had been damn good at hiding the evidence. I figured, it was probably a little bit of both.

A gust of hot wind blasted me, whipping my hair into a frenzy. I let my hair flap and felt the wind on my neck and skin, relishing the feeling. I figured the thing inside was relishing the feeling, too. Through me. Sensing the physical world again through me.

So, we both sat there on the rock, enjoying the night breeze, as the nocturnal creatures came out, although not as many this high up, above the treeline with little vegetation. Still, I heard the scurrying, the scratching, the vocalizing. It was late fall and I should have been cold. I wasn't.

Of course, I had a good bead on who was stalking the hikers up here. Nancy wasn't lying to me. She believed what she was telling me. Whether or not her ex-boyfriend was killing the hikers—or that he was, in fact, a werewolf—remained to be seen.

I closed my eyes and felt the wind ripple my clothing and rock me gently. I rested my hands on my knees and let my mind slip away, far away from here. Where it went, I didn't know, but there on the mountaintop, far from anyone and anything, I found a rare moment of peace.

And I treasured it.

Then, when I was back, I opened my eyes, took a deep and useless breath, and then did what any other lost girl would do on a mountaintop.

I stripped off all my clothing and used a much-honed technique of wrapping my clothes, including my shoes, inside my shirt and tying it all together with the legs of my jeans. Just add a stick through it, and I could have been a hobo.

Then I summoned the single flame and saw the giant creature I would soon become.

A moment later, in a process that was painless, unlike in the movies, I was very much not just another lost girl. I was something monstrous and far too scary for this world.

Using a clawed foot, I hooked my makeshift traveling satchel, gathered myself there on the rocky outcropping, and then launched high into the sky...

And spread my wings wide.

Now, I thought, as I caught a hot gust of wind and sailed out over a dark valley, *Where did I park my car...?*

14.

We were in bed.

It was past midnight, and the evening had been invigorating. Thanks to my little tirade last year—a tirade which involved the impaling of Kingsley's hand with a fork—we had been forced to look for a new hangout. We had found it by way of The Cellar restaurant in downtown Fullerton. More accurately, *under* downtown Fullerton, as the name was indeed fitting. It was also underneath the offices of our local congressman, which, I think, might have been cooler than it really was.

The Cellar was more our style. Dark, gloomy, isolated. I probably still couldn't get away with impaling Kingsley, but at least we could probably sneak back in.

Afterward, we had walked around downtown Fullerton, holding hands, looking in windows, avoiding drunks and rowdy college students, often one and the same. It was, after all, a Friday night and nearby Fullerton College was in full swing. Harbor Boulevard was lined with white lights, in a sort of year-round Christmas décor. We walked past Jacky's gym, which was presently dark, other than a small, muted glow in the back offices. Maybe Jacky was going over the books.

Spirit activity was everywhere. Downtown Fullerton was particularly old for Southern California. Lots of activity here over the years, lots of death and crime, too. Lots of heart attacks and car accidents and muggings. In fact, one such accident kept replaying itself, over and over, on a nearby street corner. Two cars coming together in an explosion of light. Over and over. I watched three spirits separate from the wreckage and stand together, looking down and looking confused.

Kingsley saw the spirits, too, but rarely let them get to him, and never did he feel a need to help the truly lost souls. Early on, I had. I wanted to go to each one, and urge them to move on. To the light, and all of that. But I have since come to realize that I can't help them all.

And the truth is...

Well, the truth is, I am caring less and less these days about whether they move on or not. Their plight is not my plight. I have my own issues. Yes, I know some of the uncaring was coming from *her* within me. Then again, it was because of her that I could even see the damn spirits in the first place.

After our stroll—and after Kingsley had tossed aside a young punk who had pinned a girl to a wall and had been talking to her a little too aggressively —we had made our way back to his place.

Once there, and once Franklin had taken our coats, we somehow, magically, ended up in his bedroom. From there, the clothing was optional... and mostly optional.

Thirty minutes later, the big oaf lifted himself off me. Damn good thing I didn't have to breathe. Afterward, we had gotten a midnight snack and eaten it over his kitchen counter. I was wearing his long shirt. He was wearing no shirt. While we talked, I might have giggled one too many times, because Franklin had appeared in the doorway, looking none too pleased. Then again, he rarely looked pleased to see me. Of course, he also sported a scar that literally wrapped around his neck. A scar that implied, well, that he'd lost his head at some point.

Someday, I would get Kingsley to open up about Franklin.

Anyway, we both apologized to the patchwork butler. Franklin sneered, turned his head, and loped away. That one leg seemed longer than the other or that one ear was actually a different skin tone than the other, was disturbing.

Now, back up in his room, I lay next to Kingsley, with one hand propping up my head and the other veritably buried in his chest hair.

"I get that you are a werewolf," I started. "I also get that you change each full moon. I even get that you play host to your own highly evolved dark master, as do I. What I don't get is why you are so damn hairy."

"It goes back to what I said a while back, Sam."

"That you continue to grow."

"With each transformation, I'm just that much bigger. That much closer to the beast within."

"And that much hairier?"

"In short, yes," he said. "Will that be a problem?"

I didn't have to think about it. "It won't be a problem for me," I said. "But I can't vouch for your shower drains."

"One of Franklin's many jobs is maintaining the household plumbing. Let's just say, I keep him busy."

"Eww."

He laughed and pulled me into him. I don't think I could have resisted him if I tried. Instead, I went willingly, and found my face buried somewhere between his shoulder and neck... a good place to be.

"You are too much," he said.

"I'd like to think so."

We were quiet some more. I heard Kingsley's late-night snack rumbling in his belly—his had been a roast beef sandwich, mine had been sherbet ice cream. After a moment, I said, "When you had sex with mortals in the past, did they, you know, fall under your spell, too?"

"The way the boxer did with you?"

"Yes, and he has a name."

"Any man who had sex with you ceases to have a name. They are no-names, at that point."

"Fine. Yes, the boxer."

"No. Not that I know of. That particular spell might be Samantha Moon-centric."

"Meaning?"

"Meaning, it's particular to the entity within you."

That gave me pause for thought. As I paused and as I thought, I discovered that I was making curlicues in Kingsley's chest hair. He didn't seem to mind. I said, "So, you're saying that not all vampires have the same powers?"

He shook his granite-like head slowly. I think the whole damn bed shook with it. "Nor do all werewolves. We all have similar traits, true. All werewolves change at the full moon. But not all werewolves, for instance, can change at will."

"Like you can," I said.

He nodded. "But not all talents are gifts, Sam. The entity within me craves the dead."

"You mean corpses," I said.

"Yes, Sam. The fucking sick bastard literally gets off on it."

"Jesus."

"Jesus is right," said Kingsley. "Which brings up a point. Some vampires can see themselves in mirrors, others can't."

"I can't," I said.

"I know. Some vampires can turn into mice, into fog, others can climb sheer walls."

"You know a lot about vampires for being a wolfie."

"We are not that dissimilar, Sam. We're all possessed by the same dark forces."

"I love when you sweet talk me," I said.

"There's more," he said, taking in a lot of air and propping his free hand under his head. I almost felt sorry for his hand...and pillow. "Some vampires prefer living humans. Some prefer dead."

"Mine prefers the living," I said. "Of course, she can prefer all she wants. She gets what she gets."

"And that brings up another point. In the end, we all have some semblance of free will. For instance, I can cage the creature within me, thus depriving him of fresh corpses. And quit shuddering every time I say that."

I shuddered again.

"Jesus, Sam. We are grown adults here, dealing with the same shit."

"Sorry," I said, patting his meaty chest. "I'll do my best to get used to the thought of you chowing down on the dead."

He rolled his eyes, which I saw clearly enough in the dark.

"None of us asked for this," he said.

"Some did," I thought.

"Fang?"

"Right."

Kingsley nodded. "Someday, he will wish that he hadn't. You still talk to him?"

I nodded. "Yeah."

"How often?"

"Regularly."

"How often is regularly?"

"Almost every day," I said.

"Oh, brother. Should I be worried?"

"No. We're friends again."

"Like old times?"

"Almost," I said. Fang had sort of gone off the deep end in the months following his transformation. In fact, his hedonistic lifestyle could have been lifted from the pages of every Anne Rice novel ever, with a little Poppy Z. Brite added in for good measure. He had lovers coming and going. He feasted on whoever and whatever he wanted. He stole, he robbed, he worked with real criminals.

It took him about a year to get it out of his system. And he had, thank God. He still ran a blood ring, but he'd ditched most of his loser business associates. Now, he mostly operated it alone and, as far as I could tell, he mostly didn't kill anyone.

The good news was, he was back to living alone, with only the occasional girlfriend showing up. What I didn't tell Kingsley was, of course, that I suspected Fang had cleaned up his life...for me.

Fang also understood that I was in a relationship with Kingsley, and had mostly kept his distance, only occasionally dropping hints that he might want more.

"Well, that's good," said the werewolf in bed next to me. "Because I will rip his head off if he makes a move on you."

"You mean that metaphorically, right?"

Kingsley grunted.

I laughed nervously and patted his chest. The truth was, I wanted to be right here, in Kingsley's arms—and nestled in that warm nook between his shoulder and jaw.

Shortly, I was asleep...and I dreamed of nothing.

Which wasn't necessarily a bad thing.

15.

It was the strangest popping sound. Like hundreds of soap bubbles bursting at once. I was just turning to see what the hell it was when I heard, "Your son is very skilled."

I gasped, mostly because no one had been standing next to me just a few seconds ago. I was certain of it. Somehow, I managed to calmly turn and look at whoever was standing next to me, whoever had managed to sneak up on even me, which, I was certain, was virtually impossible to do.

"It's you," I said.

"It is me, yes," said the man I instantly recognized. "Is this section of the mat taken?"

"No," I said before realizing that I probably should have said yes. Not that it mattered. Any man who could sneak up on me—and the Librarian, too, for that matter—was going to talk to me whether I wanted to or not.

The man nodded and I almost—almost—sensed that he could read my mind. He was dressed a little too nicely for a boxing gym. Hell, a little too nice for Fullerton, in general. His black suit was immaculate, if not a little dated. His thick black hair was slicked back with some sort of oiled wax—Brylcreem maybe—and combed perfectly. Although his clothing and hairstyle seemed a little dated, there was nothing old-fashioned about the brightness in his eyes. They flashed over me quickly and appreciatively, and he made a show of sitting down by unbuttoning his jacket and flipping up the longish tails as he sat. I had a mental image of a maestro taking a lunch break.

As he sat, I caught sight of his claw-like fingernails. I also sensed the impenetrable wall around his thoughts and a distinct lack of an aura.

He was a vampire, and, I suspected, a very old one.

He sat smoothly, in one fluid motion, his narrow limbs coming to sharp points. In fact, he didn't use his hands at all. He dropped down, legs folding under him neatly, like a collapsible picnic table. If I didn't know any better, I would have said he glided down.

Meanwhile, in front of me, my son danced in the ring with Jacky. Granted, Jacky wasn't doing much dancing these days, but he kept pace with my son, using the punching mitts, urging my son to keep his hands up. My son, for his part, seemed to revel in the workout. Heck, he even seemed to enjoy Jacky's good-natured verbal abuse. Once, after a flurry of devastating punches, he reached over and ruffled the Irishman's gray hair, to the old man's surprise and, I believe, delight. This got a swift condemnation from Jacky, but they did pause, and I caught the two of them laughing in the corner of the ring a moment later.

"Your son has phenomenal control and power," said the man sitting next to me. He had an accent that I couldn't quite place. Then again, I'd always been crappy with accents.

"Long story," I said.

"I would like to hear it someday," said the man.

I shot him a look. And the more I looked, the more I could see the fire blazing just behind his pupil. It was, I was certain, the brightest fire I'd seen yet. What that meant, I didn't know. But there it was, a single flame leaping and crackling and snapping. I should have found it distracting, except I found it to be the exact opposite.

I found it hypnotic.

So, I shifted my gaze to his long, slender nose. I had to. I felt myself...slipping into his own flames. So strange. I said, "You assume I'll see you again or that I'll want to talk to you."

"Perhaps I was loose with my speech."

I forced myself to look at my son. My warning bells had been ringing steadily, although not very loudly. There was danger here...but not immediate. I said, without looking at him, "You also presume that I care about what you like."

"And you don't?"

"I could give a fuck about what you like."

He threw back his head and laughed loudly. Except... except no one looked at him. No one but me.

"I can see why Elizabeth was keen on you, Samantha Moon. You remind me so much of her. In fact, you look quite a bit like her."

I glanced at him. "Elizabeth?"

"Don't you know?" he asked, raising a single narrow eyebrow. His sharp elbows rested lightly on his equally sharp knees.

"Know what?"

"Ah, I see her son hasn't yet shared her name with you."

The flames inside his pupil danced and wavered and sputtered as if a wind were rattling around inside his skull.

"That's her name..."

"Indeed," said the man.

"Her name is Elizabeth..." I heard myself say. Hearing her name had a strange effect on me. It...humanized her. I wasn't sure I wanted her humanized. I preferred to think of her as a demon. It was bad enough that I thought her son was kind of cute.

"And a fine name it is."

The entity within me responded to her name,

and came rushing to the surface of my thoughts, but I shut a mental lid on her before she got too far, or could take too much control.

"And who are you?" I asked.

But the man next to me seemed to guess what I was about to ask, for he was already standing and giving me a small bow. He tipped a non-existent hat, and said, in a rolling, sing-song voice, "Wladislaus Dragwlya, at your service."

Coming from him, coupled with his strange accent, the "W" sounded like a "V" to my ears.

In fact, I was certain he had said... *Vladislaus Dracula.*

16.

I caught myself rocking a little and breathing hard, although there was no damn good reason why I was breathing hard. It was a reaction, I knew. A reaction to yet the further absurdness that was my life. That had been my life for the past nine years.

While I breathed and rocked and tried to process, the man continued to watch me sideways, sitting completely still. The fire behind his pupils seemed almost palpable, to radiate real heat. But I knew that was not true. Vampires were cold, were they not?

My son took a short breather, although he barely seemed to breathe hard. Jacky, however, staggered away from the heavy bag. The poor guy literally didn't know what had hit him. First me, then my son. He must have thought we were the freakiest of freaks.

Not the freakiest, I thought. *In fact, the original freak was sitting next to me now.*

Dracula.

I forcibly calmed myself. After all, had I not met other vampires? Hell, I had encountered werewolves, angels and body-hopping demons. Wasn't he just another...

No, he wasn't.

He was fucking Dracula and, according to the Librarian, the original vampire. The first vampire. The oldest vampire.

Jesus...

"You seem upset, Samantha Moon."

"Wouldn't you be?" I said. "If, you know, you just met you. Okay, that sounded lame."

He threw back his head and laughed easily. "Yes," he finally said when the laughter subsided. "I suppose I would be upset, too, if, you know, I had just met me."

For the first time in a long time, I felt embarrassed, although my face didn't burn with embarrassment. To do so would have implied that I radiated some degree of heat, which I didn't. Not like the creature next to me.

Confused, I shut my mouth and might have rocked a little. We lapsed into silence, although the thoughts in my head weren't so silent. And the demon bitch inside me wasn't helping either. She was clamoring to get out. It was all I could do to stamp her back down and throw up a mental wall, which was harder to do than it sounds, especially when you've got something living in you...and that something desperately wants out. Months ago, I had learned that I didn't like communicating with her directly. Despite what the Librarian had told me last year, love didn't seem to be working. She only seemed to be getting angrier or more desperate. Then again, maybe she was getting angrier and more desperate because of love. Either way, she had made my life a living nightmare.

"Why are you here?" I asked.

"Isn't it obvious?"

"You want to take boxing lessons?"

He laughed again, the sound coming from him surprisingly easily. I would never have guessed that Dracula had such a good sense of humor, other than, say, laughing maniacally as he watched those being impaled before him: men, women and children. Indeed, Dracula had been a monster before he became a monster.

"Not quite, Samantha, although I see your friend Jacky is quite gifted."

I was disturbed by his knowledge of my name and Jacky's. He undoubtedly knew my son's name, too. He'd been following me, for how long, I didn't know.

"So, why are you here?"

"I thought it was time to make my presence known."

"And I care, why?"

He didn't laugh at my abruptness this time. Instead, his eyes narrowed and I caught a brief glimpse of the monster he was. Something flashed behind his eyes, something that did not approve of being talked to in such a way. I could give a fuck about what he approved and didn't approve, Dracula or not.

"Because we are connected, Samantha Moon."

"I beg to differ."

"You can feel her reaching out to me, can't you?"

"Not you," I said. "The thing within you."

"Myself and the thing within me...are very much the same, Samantha, as we have been for many centuries. Call it an equal partnership."

"I call it creepy as hell."

"Perhapsss..."

I shivered at that. Indeed, I was sensing that Dracula and the demon within were interchangeable, coming and going at will, one rising to the surface, while the other stepped back, almost instantly. Perhaps they existed side-by-side, if that was possible.

"What do you want from me?" I asked.

"You know what we want, Sssamantha."

"Yeah, well, you ain't getting her. So, you can both go to hell."

The man, known as Vlad Tepes, who had killed tens of thousands of the innocent back in the day, whose name was synonymous with evil, smiled at me slowly. "Do not be so quick to dismiss us,

Sssamantha. We can offer you much."

"You have nothing I want—"

His movement was instant, certainly faster than I could react. One moment his hands were folded in his lap, and the next, he was holding my own hand, gripping it tightly. I tried to rise, but he held me in place.

"Do you feel that, Sam?"

"Let go, asshole, or this is going to get ugly."

"Do you feel my warmth, Sam? Do you? This could be yours again. This, and so much more."

"Let me fucking go."

"No one can see me, Sam. They think you are talking to yourself."

I stopped struggling and looked around. Indeed, others in the gym were staring at me, including my son and Jacky, who had stopped their recent round of workouts.

"I don't understand," I said under my breath.

"I will explain everything to you, Samantha. This and so much more. Every secret. Everything."

"Let go," I said, "or I will tear your fucking throat out."

Vlad Tepes held my gaze, and released my hand. "Consider my words."

"Go to hell."

"I'll be back," he said.

He smiled, stood, and walked away, exiting the gym and heading out into the night.

17.

"It looks closed, Ma," said Anthony.

He was right, of course. In fact, the whole damn campus looked closed. No surprise there, since it was Friday night, the only night the school's epic library closed early.

I might have growled under my breath. The Librarian and his damn inconvenient hours. Where he went when the library was closed, I hadn't a clue. But I was going to find him and talk to him, dammit.

A handful of students milled about, some alone, some walking with friends, others standing around and making plans for the weekend. Some lights were on in some of the buildings, but for the most part, the place was closed for business.

Anthony and I stood at the library's front entrance, whose automatic doors normally whispered open. There was no whispering now. Inside, through the smoke glass, the place was dark and empty, save for a dim light hanging over the help desk inside.

"So, Jacky thinks I'll be ready soon..." continued Anthony. My boy had been talking non-stop since we'd left his practice session with Jacky.

"Uh-huh," I said and led him around to the side of the massive structure. Anthony trotted along, pretty much oblivious to his surroundings, so wrapped up was he in his story.

"But he says I gotta keep practicing my footwork."

And to show me what he meant—or just to get some extra reps in—he did just that. His sneakered feet moved rapidly over the wet grass, crossing and scissoring. As they moved, my son moved his shoulders, too, dodging an invisible assailant, moving faster than he had any right to move.

No, I thought, *he has every right.*

He was, after all, now acting as his own guardian angel.

Craziness, I thought. *All of this.*

We were now standing under a floodlight next to the library, where no mom and son belong. So, before anyone spotted us, I grabbed hold of his juking and jiving shoulders—which was no easy feat—and led my son out of the light and over into the shadows.

"Fly like a butterfly, sting like a bee!" he said, still moving his feet this way and that.

"I'm going to sting your butt like a bee if you don't keep it down," I said, whispering.

"But Mom..."

"Don't 'but Mom' me," I said. "We're going to break into the library and I don't want any backtalk."

"But...wait, did you say we're going to break into the library?"

"I did," I said, then knelt down and turned around. I motioned to my back. "Climb on, kiddo."

"But I'm almost as big as you."

"Anthony..."

"Fine, but if I break your back, then that's on you, not me."

As he climbed on, I considered leaving him here in the shadows...but then shook my head sharply. Hell, no. Meeting the King Creep had freaked me out completely and totally...and I needed more answers, and I needed them now.

"Hang on," I said, standing.

And with my son's long legs dangling down on either side of me, I took hold of the drainpipe and started climbing.

Rapidly.

18.

Twenty seconds later, we slipped in through a third-story window that had been left cracked open. I cracked it all the way open. There was no fire escape or ledge, and whoever had left it open hadn't expected someone to climb three stories up a drainpipe. With her son hanging off her back, no less.

"This is cool, Mom!" said Anthony, when he slid off and found his feet.

"Shh!"

"Oh, right. Sorry."

We found ourselves in an administrator's office, complete with a blinking monitor and a glow-in-the-dark keyboard and mouse and a small, gurgling fountain that was presently running. Wasteful.

"Come on," I whispered.

The office led to a hallway, lined with many doors. The halogen lighting above was off. The floor was polished vinyl squares. I led the way down the hallway toward an "Exit" sign hanging over another door.

I already knew that my son hadn't inherited my night vision, which was, apparently, primarily a vampire and werewolf trait. The angel had only bestowed upon him great strength, agility and quickness.

Good enough, I thought.

I paused at the door at the far end of the hallway and pressed my ear against it. Nothing. I was fairly certain the door would lead to the main library on the third floor. I turned the knob and cracked the door open a smidgen...

I heard a door bang open, followed by the sounds of running feet. Many running feet. Security guards approached, and from the sounds of it, at least three of them. So much for sneaking in.

I turned to my son. "Do *not* tell your sister about this."

"Oh, I won't."

"Or your auntie."

"My friends?"

"No," I said. "This stays between me and you."

"Fine," he said, and flashed me a giddy smile.

"Are you ready to run?" I asked, as the voices and pounding footsteps got closer.

"Yes!"

And run we did, exploding out of the doorway and hanging a quick right down a side corridor, where we ran along the west wall. The Occult Reading Room was on the south wall.

"This way!" someone shouted behind us.

"Faster," I said to my son, and we kicked into a whole other gear. Bookshelves swept past us in a blur. I looked back once and saw my son keeping up with me virtually step for step, although I was pulling away. I slowed down and let him catch up. Then we made a quick left. The Occult Reading Room was about halfway down the south corridor.

A bobbing flashlight was directly ahead. Someone was running toward us. I reached back and took my son's hand.

Unlike the movies, I didn't just appear somewhere when I ran. I actually had to cover some ground. I had to pass through time and space. There was no movie magic here. Just my son, me, and a security guard, all converging at or around the Occult Reading Room.

We were too far away for him to see us, although I'm sure he heard our pounding footsteps. Our furiously pounding footsteps. The guy probably didn't know what was coming at him.

"Hang on," I said to my son.

As we rapidly approached the security guard, who dropped his flashlight and held up what appeared to be a Taser gun, I hung a hard right through a narrow doorway, pulling my son with me.

The security guard screamed. So did my son. I didn't blame either of them.

***

Worst mom ever, I thought.

"It's okay," I said, hugging my son. "We're safe."

"But he's right—"

"He can't see us. This is a secret room."

"Secret?"

"Yes."

"Like magic?"

"Exactly like magic," I said.

Outside, through windows that only my son and I could see, we watched the confused security guard sweep his light over the wall. Each time, my son ducked, until he started getting the picture that the guard couldn't see us.

Still the worst mom ever, I thought.

More security guards appeared, each sweeping their light over the area while the first guard did his damnedest to explain what had happened.

"They went through here," he said, and now he sounded like he was doubting himself. He should doubt himself. To all the world, "there" was just a blank wall.

"They went through *where*?" asked another guard.

The first guy pointed his light right at us. My son's previous reaction was to duck, but this time, he held firm, standing his ground. "Right here. Through this wall."

All the flashlights hit the wall at once.

"It's a wall, Mick—"

"I swear to God—"

This went on for another half minute, until one of them got the bright idea that there was a chance that we went left instead of right. And so, they dashed off down a side corridor, flashlights bobbing and pounding footsteps receding.

I felt the presence behind us before he spoke. "You certainly know how to make an entrance, Samantha Moon."

19.

I got my son settled in one of the reading chairs, where he was doing just that: reading.

No, he wasn't brushing up on his dark magic or even studying for his potions finals with Severus Snape. No, he was using the Kindle app on my iPhone to plow through *The Hunger Games* trilogy, reading like there was no tomorrow. And, according to *The Hunger Games*, tomorrow looked bleak indeed.

Anyway, I'd admonished him to not touch anything, under any circumstances. He had agreed with a wave of his hand, face aglow in the phone's back light. What chance did I have to compete with Katniss Everdeen?

At the Help Desk, Maximus, who was wearing a

tee-shirt and sweats, said, "You are annoyed at me."

"Pissed would be a better word. You didn't warn me that Dracula himself would come looking for me someday."

"And if I had, what would that have accomplished, other than to make you nervous? To make you jump at the slightest shadow? There was and is no way to prevent him from seeking you."

"Well, he did, and he found me, and it freaked me the fuck out."

"I imagine so. Would you mind if I relived the experience, Sam?"

"Relive away," I said. "But I'm still pissed at you."

Maximus sighed and came over to my side of the help desk...and then helped himself to my memories. By helping, I meant he placed his hands on my head and asked me to relax and to go back to when I first saw the Count, as I was now affectionately referring to him. Anyway, I did go back to when the creepy bastard first appeared in the gym. I then relived the conversation as best as I could remember. A few minutes later, Max pulled away.

The alchemist blinked rapidly, then made his way back to his side of the Help Desk. "He can appear and disappear."

"You can say that again," I said.

"And yet, when he was here in the Reading Room, I didn't see him. And when he laughed loudly in the boxing ring...no one turned to look."

"What are you getting at?" I asked.

"I don't actually know," he said. "But he seems to have the ability to project himself where he wants. Then again, you are the only one who seems to see him."

"Yay," I said. "So, what does that mean?"

"I think," said the Alchemist. "I think he can project an aspect of himself, seen only by you. Or, if not just by you, perhaps others of his kind."

"You mean vampires?"

"Yes."

"But am I seeing him, or a part of him?"

"I don't know," said Maximus, "but this adds a new wrinkle to stopping him."

"So, you're saying this bastard can literally appear to me anywhere, at any time of the day."

"So it appears."

That thought alone made me want to run to the diamond medallion, which would, according to Max, remove the entity from within me. Except the entity within me wanted to attach herself to my bloodline. And a female bloodline at that. Leaving my sister—and even my daughter—the next in line for them to attack. I had a thought.

"Couldn't you just make other diamond medallions?" I asked, knowing the alchemist was more than likely following my thoughts anyway. "One for myself, and for my sister and daughter?"

"You would risk having your sister attacked? Or your daughter? And what if neither of them were able to control my mother? What if she took hold of them early on, possessed them fully, and fled to parts unknown?"

I shuddered at the thought. He was right, of course. The best way to manage—or control—his mother was, for now, through me.

Again, *yay.*

"It's easy to see the bad, Sam. I know that. Having something dark and angry living inside you cannot be fun. But try to see the good in this, if possible. I think, perhaps, that is your only saving grace."

"She doesn't want me to see the good," I said.

"Of course not. Seeing the good keeps her at bay. Seeing the good empowers you and disempowers her. Seeing the good, in effect, keeps her locked up, where she belongs. Remember always that letting her out, even for a moment, would be far, far worse."

"How bad?" I asked.

"Madness, perhaps. Or worse."

"Worse than madness?"

The Librarian shrugged, and I considered again the man known as Vlad Tepes, which, I now knew meant Vlad the Impaler. Had he gone mad...or was he already mad? He didn't seem mad. He seemed keen...aware. He seemed, above all, stable and in control of himself. That was, of course, until the entity had spoken through him.

"There's no knowing their relationship," said the Librarian, following my trail of thoughts easily enough. "And there's no knowing the extent of

Cornelius' possession of Vlad, either."

"It has a name?"

"Yes, Sam. Just as my mother has a name."

At the sound of it, the entity within me—Elizabeth—perked up noticeably. I had a mental image of her fighting against her restraints. She could fight all she wanted.

Max went on, "I've sometimes wondered if Cornelius had bitten off more than he could chew."

"What do you mean?" I asked.

"Vlad might have been a bigger psychopath than even Cornelius. That Vlad might have, in fact, been on the road to mastery himself."

"But I thought all the dark masters had been banned," I said. "Run out of Dodge, so to speak. By your mentor, Hermes."

"And so they had, but it is possible some had slipped through our fingers. Or, in the case of Dracula, someone who was close to being one, but not quite there."

"And how would he, Dracula, know of this Occult Reading Room?" I asked. "I thought only those who needed the room—or were ready for it—could find it?"

"A good question, Sam," said Maximus. "My guess? He's been following you for quite some time...and saw you slip in here often enough. Such hidden rooms—magical rooms, as you explained to your son—would not be unfamiliar to Cornelius, the entity within Dracula."

"And he followed me how?"

"Dracula is a shape-shifter with the best of them, Sam. He is purported to turn into fog when convenient."

"And mice," I added, recalling my teen years reading Stoker.

"Exactly."

I chewed on that for a moment. Chewed a lot. Didn't like it. Wanted to spit it the hell out. Where was a spittoon when you needed one? I said, "So, you're telling me you're not sure who is controlling whom."

"Exactly, Sam. Cornelius was and is a force to be reckoned with, second only to my mother. But Vlad..."

"Vlad is a whole other kind of crazy."

"Exactly. One the most fierce—and feared—rulers the world has ever known."

"They make for interesting bedfellows," I said, and was fairly certain that was the first time I had ever said the word "bedfellows."

"Indeed, Sam. Potentially, they are unstopp-able."

"Unstoppable from what?" I asked.

"Whatever it is they want. Which, in this case, is to open the veil between worlds."

"Um, what?"

"The veil," he said. "Between worlds."

"Oh, right," I said. "That veil. Silly me. And this is a veil that Hermes himself created."

"Created and sealed," he said.

"And I happen to be a descendent of Hermes," I

said.

"Yes."

"And where is he now?" I asked. "Seems like we could use him again."

"Hermes is gone," said Max, and I suspected we had hit upon a sore spot for him. *He misses him,* I thought. Maximus held my gaze for a moment, then looked away.

"Gone where?" I asked.

"I don't really know, Sam. There are other worlds out there. Other people who need help. You have experienced these other worlds with the creature known as Talos, who lives in such alternate worlds."

"You're making my head spin," I said.

"Sorry, Sam. But such highly evolved masters as Hermes Trismegistus aren't long for our world. They're needed elsewhere."

"To fight other dark masters."

"Indeed, Sam. But he would never use words such as 'fight.' He saw it as maintaining balance."

"So, he would go to worlds that were out of balance?"

"Something like that."

"And our world is balanced now?"

"It had been, Sam. For the past five hundred years."

"And now?" I asked.

"Now," said Archibald Maximus, "I don't know. But Hermes did not leave us without hope."

"Oh?"

"He left behind his bloodline. A very powerful bloodline. I think you see where I'm going with this."

"I do," I said. "And I think you might see me curl up in the fetal position any moment now."

He laughed lightly. "You are more powerful than you know, Sam. And you are not alone. Not ever."

I was just about to tell him a fat lot of good that did me, when my son screamed bloody murder.

20.

What I saw shouldn't have surprised me.

A thick book lay open on the floor, black smoke billowing up from its yellowed pages. My son was shrinking away in fear...and screaming for his mom.

I dashed through the reading room, nearly flying, and swept my son up into my arms and watched in amazement as the swirling, twisting smoke morphed into a monstrous, undulating, amorphous snake. Now it wove throughout the room, just above our heads. It moved and slithered and my son whimpered in my arms, burying his face into my shoulders.

I didn't blame him. I found myself ducking from the flying, circling serpent, a serpent that seemed to only grow bigger and bigger, expanding exponentially. It also took on mass, shifting from something smoky and ill-defined, to sprouting actual scales and fangs, and two black eyes...and a flicking tongue.

Now I heard it, too. A harsh whisper, a sound that seemed to fill the room, or perhaps just my head.

"Yesss, yesss, yesss..."

Bigger it grew, until, I suspected, it was going to bust out of this very room. I found myself ducking with each passing, with each flicking of its forked tongue. My hair billowed in its slipstream.

Amazingly, Max stepped *through* it. As he did so, its slithering, coiling body exploded, then reformed again in the air above us. The young alchemist raised his hands and whispered words I could not understand—hell, words that I did not want to understand.

The flying serpent circled faster and faster. Its tongue flicked. It undulated and grew. Its black eyes were watching me, watching everything. Now its huge jaws opened wide and it struck at the alchemist's head. I was ready to spring into action, but he didn't need me. Indeed, he waved off the attack with a swipe of his hand, and the snake's head momentarily exploded into smoke, and then reformed itself. Bigger than ever.

"Yesss, yesss, yesss..."

Now, Max was no longer mumbling. Indeed, he spoke loudly and rapidly and with commanding authority. I still couldn't make out the words. I still didn't want to make out the words.

But something was happening. The snake was slowing down. It was also shrinking. The wind in the room was decreasing, too.

"Nooo..." it hissed. *"Nooo..."*

A moment later, I watched the rapidly-diminishing creature return to smoke vapor...and reverse back into the book from whence it came. Its anguished cries disappeared with it.

When it was gone, the ancient book slammed shut on its own.

21.

It was much later.

Too late for a mom to be talking to her son about demons, black magic and cursed grimoires. But here I was, doing exactly that. Not to mention, my son wouldn't let me leave his side, which was why I was now lying in bed next to him, running my fingers through his hair. Periodically, he would convulse and shake so violently that his teeth would rattle.

Each time he did so, I hated myself more and more.

We'd been lying like this for the past two hours. I kept waiting for Anthony to drift to sleep, but he hadn't yet. Every so often, he let out a pitiful, cat-like mew that broke my heart into a thousand pieces. My son had been reduced to a frightened, shivering newborn kitten, and it had been all my fault. Not to mention, he kept apologizing, over and over, which he did again now.

"I'm so sorry, Mommy," he said into his pillow, and the words came out hoarse and barely discernible.

"It's not your fault, baby."

"But I let it out, Mommy. It was all my fault."

Again, I told him it wasn't and patted him and quietly wiped tears from my cheeks with my free hand. It was all I could do to not cry in front of my son. I knew that it was important to be strong for him now. He needed to know that his mother could protect him...from anything.

"Mommy," he asked after a few minutes, "what *was* that thing?"

I knew exactly what it was. The Librarian had filled me in, and now I considered just how much to tell my boy. I decided not too much.

"It was something that can't hurt you, baby. Not now. Not ever."

"It asked me for help."

He had told me this a dozen times before, but I let him get it out again, if he needed to.

"I didn't know what it was. I know you told me not to touch anything, and not to listen to anything, but I..."

"I know, baby."

"I guess I wasn't expecting something to ask me for help...and it was coming from a book."

"I know—"

"A book, Mom. Do you know how crazy that is?"

"About as crazy as it gets."

"You were so busy talking to Max, and he was holding your head like you had a headache or something, and all I did was open the book..." His voice trailed off and he whimpered again.

I knew what happened next, of course. The voice had asked him to repeat a word or two. And my son had...and that had been all the demon needed.

At the time, I had been worried that something else might have happened, that somehow, my son had gotten possessed, but the Librarian had waved it off, insisting the demon was back where it belonged, sealed within the book. Still, I had him check out my son, although I wasn't sure what we were looking for. Max had given my son a clean bill of health—or, rather, a clean bill of *possession-free* health.

Another hour of whimpering and patting and mewing later, my son finally turned to me and said, "I'll be okay now, Mommy. You can go to bed now. Or go to work. Or whatever it is you do all night."

I smiled and kissed him on his warm forehead.

Two hours later, after finishing up some work in my office and clearing out my email—I always wondered what people thought about getting emails from me at 3:28 in the morning—I found myself standing in the open doorway of my son's bedroom, watching him sleep, relieved all over again that all seemed to be well.

That had been close, and scary as hell, even for me.

I was about to turn away—about to get some shuteye of my own—when my son rolled over onto his side...

And looked directly at me.

Except, he wasn't looking.

He was staring.

I blinked, sure I was seeing things—and when I opened them again, his eyes were closed and he was sleeping soundly.

Rattled—and apparently still shaken from the night's events—I headed off to bed.

22.

I couldn't sleep.

And since dawn was still a few hours away, I stripped down in the shadows of my backyard orange tree, and transformed into something giant and alien and most definitely out of this world.

For those unlucky few, they would have seen a giant, hulking creature leap from the shadows of my back yard...and straight up into the sky, flapping its huge, leathery wings hard.

Now, I followed the coastline, which was always my favorite route. The cresting waves foamed and glowed under the quarter moon. The full moon was just under a week or so away.

When the werewolves play.

Well, some of them, at least. According to

Kingsley, most werewolves tended to stay indoors and locked down, which made sense, since there really weren't a lot of "vicious wild animal attacks" reported in Southern California.

There were, of course, dozens and dozens of missing persons in California...and just about everywhere else, too.

Kingsley called tonight and, in much coded language, had let me know that little was known about Gunther Kessler in the werewolf community. Kingsley suggested, in even more coded language (he never liked talking about this stuff over the phone), that many of his wolfie friends had been somewhat guarded when he approached them about Gunther. This confused Kingsley. He'd never known his friends to be guarded. He didn't know what to make of it, and neither did I, although he told me again, for the umpteenth time, to be careful.

I flapped lazily, continuously.

I could have been a giant manta ray, sailing through the heavens. What I was, exactly, was not clear. I knew a creature from another world was summoned to be exchanged with my own body. A sort of parallel universe swap. I knew that my own body would be resting comfortably—and, hopefully, safely—in this other world. Presently, I did not have access to my human body, wherever it was. At least, I hadn't figured out how to have access to it yet. Talos, on the other hand, *did* have access to his body here on Earth, a body he permitted me to take over completely.

Could I die in his world? I didn't know. Could Talos die in our world? It was hard to say. I knew Talos could kill in our world, as we had done together on that remote Washington island, years ago.

It was, of course, enough to make my head spin.

We are together, and we are separate, Samantha Moon, came a deep voice inside me. And not just inside my head. It seemed to surround me, fill me. *Your world is not used to the concept of duality. Or, rather unwilling to accept it.*

Well, hello, Talos, I thought. *Fancy meeting you here.*

An earth idiom, I assume.

You assume correctly, I thought.

Your inability to understand duality is expected.

Because of the physical world we live in, I thought.

Indeed. Time and space render such concepts difficult to comprehend.

I thought: *Well, few of us—outside of our most advanced mystics—will ever fully wrap our brains around the idea that we can be in two places at once.*

And yet you are, in fact, in two places at once, Samantha Moon. I would even argue three.

You're referring to my higher self, I thought.

Indeed, Sam. The higher self or soul or the spark of the divine or whatever you choose to call it, that which is truly you exists elsewhere.

Where?

Beyond the physical, in what some would call the energetic realms.

Is that where you're from?

Close, Sam. My world is a hybrid world.

And what the devil does that mean?

Both physical and spiritual exist side by side. We have long since mastered how to be in two places at once, and sometimes three or four places.

Now my head really hurts.

Careful, thought Talos, *it's my head, too. The truth is, your world is a hybrid world, too, although your kind is slanted primarily toward the physical. But at any time, humanity could make the leap to embrace the spiritual.*

Well, don't expect that any time soon.

You might be surprised, Sam. There is greater good going on in your earth than is presently being reported.

You would think, I thought, *from the news we see that war is just around every corner.*

And is it? Is that your experience?

No, I thought. *But it's the experience of others—*

Not the vast majority of others, Sam. The truth is, a slight shift is occurring in your world as we speak. A shift toward peace.

Not if the thing within me has any say in it.

Oh, there will be a few who will fight the shift to their last breath...but their days are numbered. But do not think of this as a war, Sam. Remember what you were once told: defeat the enemy with love.

And how do you know what I was once told?

Because I am you, too, Sam. We are one in this moment.

And you have access to my memories?

In a way, yes.

And I have access to yours?

If you so choose.

I'm not sure I can handle your memories, I thought. *I kinda have a lot to juggle on my end.*

So it seems.

What is a demon? I suddenly asked.

A lost entity, one that has been lost for so long that it chooses to never, ever find itself.

Were they good once?

It's hard to say, Sam. They are from God, so, of course they were once good.

Because we're all one and all that jazz?

Exactly. But not all entities evolve. Some choose to do the opposite.

To devolve?

Something like that. But if you ask me, I secretly suspect such entities are fulfilling a role for God.

So, they were created on purpose?

Perhaps, perhaps not. I do not know. I am only postulating an hypothesis.

And since when did giant flying vampire bats postulate hypotheses?

I might be the first.

I laughed, then thought: *Perhaps they were created to be a foil?*

Or to show us darkness.

Because without darkness...

You cannot see the light, finished Talos. *But make no mistake, Samantha. Demons are real. They are powerful. And they are everywhere.*

Gee, thanks for that pick-me-up.

There was a long silence as I continued up the coast, now flying high above Santa Barbara. I would have to circle back soon, but not yet. In the far, far distance, I caught sight of something else. A shadow moving through the heavens. A shadow in the shape of a...

No, I thought. *That can't be.*

But it was, I certain of it.

It was a dragon.

23.

We were in my minivan.

I'd forgotten that this evening was "ghouls' night out" as Allison liked to call it. I'd compromised with her and now here we were on a stakeout together... and she wouldn't stop talking.

"Stakeouts," I said, "are generally done in silence."

"That was a rude thing to say, Sam. Besides, tonight was ghouls' night out—"

"Will you quit saying that?"

She continued, without missing a beat, "—and you know damn well I look forward to this night all week. Besides, it's also been a week since, you know."

Yes, I knew well. It had been a week since I'd

last fed from her wrist and I could feel the effects. A little lethargic. A little less than what I knew I could be. True, I'd drunk my fill of cow and pig blood from my supply in the garage, but it wasn't the same. That was equivalent to living on McDonald's. Eventually it wore you down and sapped your energy. Sadly, normal food didn't help. At all. I could eat ten scones from Starbucks and still feel depleted. I needed blood, and I needed it about every other day.

Yeah, a true ghoul, I thought.

I heard that, came Allison's thought.

"You caught me," I said. "And we'll take care of that later."

That being, of course, me drinking from her wrist, usually from the same old scar. Luckily for her, she healed almost instantly as soon as I pulled away from her. Vampire saliva had that effect.

We were sitting in the front seat of my minivan, parked in the same spot down the road, in front of a house that mostly appeared empty, which was why I had chosen it.

"Is he always this busy?" asked Allison.

"Not so far," I said.

Indeed, we saw the silhouette of a man— Gunther, no doubt—flashing back and forth behind the glass of his front door. We saw lights turn on and off. At one point, we heard him in the garage.

"So, what do you think he's up to?"

"Hard to know," I said.

"The full moon is in, what, three nights?"

"Two," I said. "Sunday night."

"Why don't we, you know, confront him? Before he hurts someone else?"

"And make him tell me what I need to know?"

"Well..." she thought about that. "Yeah, I guess."

"If he's a werewolf—and it's looking more and more like he is—then he'll be as strong or stronger than me. Besides, if I confront him, he could go into hiding, or disappear altogether."

"So, you're waiting to flush him out, or catch him in the act."

"Something like that."

"To think there are actually these *things* running around at full moons, hungry for people."

"Most aren't running around at full moons. Most are responsible. Most don't want to get caught. Most lead fairly normal lives and want to continue leading them."

"Like Kingsley," she said.

"Right."

"And maybe this guy, too."

"Maybe," I said.

"So, you're saying that they practice safe transforming?"

Sometimes Allison, despite her neediness and clinginess, made me laugh, which I did now. "Responsible transforming, yes."

"I can see the public service announcement now," said Allison and adopted a mock announcer voice: "Transform safely and comfortably in a padlocked cell deep beneath your home..."

"The More You Know..." I said.

Now, we were both snickering, although I really didn't feel like snickering. Not after seeing what I had seen last night: Vlad Tepes, the escaped demon, and my son staring at me, although that last one could have been my imagination. Still, the laughter felt good, and it might have been my first laughter in the last 24 hours.

When we were done, we both smiled at an old lady walking her labradoodle past our parked minivan. She gave us a good, hard look, and I waved to her and smiled. So did Allison. The old lady didn't smile back.

"She's going to be trouble," said Allison.

"Probably," I said.

"Then why don't you do your vampire-mind-trick on her? Or whatever you call it."

"I don't call it anything. Besides, I already called the Orange Police Department days ago. They know I'm in the area doing surveillance."

"Gee, you private dicks think of everything."

I was about to comment when I saw it again: a car sporting a mustache attached to its grill, driving slowly by.

"You see that?" I asked, pointing.

"What? The car with the mustache?"

"Yeah, that. What's the deal with that?"

"I don't know, but I feel like I've seen those before."

"I have, too. In fact, three of them on this very

street."

"Three different cars?"

I nodded and thought about that and nearly Googled it again when Allison suddenly turned and faced me. My friend was quite lovely. Dark hair, almond-shaped eyes, caramel skin. She reached out and took my cold hand. I flinched involuntarily, as I always do when people touch me.

"There's something about this case that you're keeping from me, Sam. Something buried so deep that I can't quite see it."

"You don't get to know all my secrets," I snapped, pulling my hand free.

Allison, to her credit, didn't take offense. She also knew that I could get pretty damn moody sometimes. She got it. She also knew when my snapping wasn't about her. Of course, having a mostly open telepathic connection helped, too.

So, instead of being hurt or snapping back, she blinked and calmly said, "Nor do I want to, Sam, but I can feel the conflict within you. It's bubbling up to your surface, then sinks down again. I've felt it ever since you took on this case."

I drummed my fingers on the steering wheel. I almost wished Gunther would make an appearance, just so I wouldn't have to answer Allison's question.

"That bad, huh?" asked Allison.

"I'm afraid so," I said, and let the full extent of my misgivings percolate to the surface of my thoughts.

"Just know that I'm here for you," she said.
"And I don't mean that in a needy way."

"Yes, you do."

"Bitch," said Allison.

Had we been guys, I might have socked her in
the arm. But we were girls so, I winked at her and
blew her a kiss and she shook her head, then grew
somber again. "So, what gives about this case?"

I drummed my nails on the steering wheel...and
decided to come clean. "I'm just having a hard time
caring," I said.

"Caring about what?"

"About catching Gunther Kessler."

"But...but you have to care, Sam."

"Why?" I asked. "Why do I have to care?"

"Didn't you take, like, an oath to care?"

"To protect and serve?"

"Yes, that."

"No. That's the police."

"But if you don't care, then you are falling into
their trap, playing right into their hands."

I drummed my fingers on the steering wheel,
fighting a feeling inside me...or, rather, trying to
understand my *lack* of feeling. My lack of caring for
the missing hikers.

It's her, I thought.

No, it's me.

I gripped the steering wheel more tightly. The
conversation was making me feel uncomfortable. I
suddenly needed some air, although air is not what I
needed, ever. I rolled down the window and got a

breeze going. The day was warm, and the street was mostly quiet. The old lady with her labradoodle was gone. For now.

I had a sudden, exciting image of breaking the old lady's neck, twisting her head so hard that she died right there in my hands, while I feasted from her spasming corpse.

"Holy shit, Sam. Please tell me you didn't just think that."

"She's asking for it."

"No, she's not, Sam. She's a concerned citizen, wondering why two women are parked on the street for hours on end."

I felt the anger rise in me. I felt a strong need to lash out at Allison for being such a stupid bitch. It took all I had to not say something horrible...and to not do something horrible either. I held my hands in my lap, interlocking my fingers, putting myself under house arrest. I rocked back and forth, releasing some of the energy.

A moment later, when I had calmed down, I heard Allison audibly exhale, too. She sensed correctly that the worst had passed. For both of us. Allison was, after all, a powerful, albeit new, witch. There was no telling what she would have done to me in return.

"That was scary, Sam."

I shook my head, looking down and rocking, rocking.

"But I think what's scariest of all is that I..." she paused, tried again. "Is that I know that was all you."

She was right, of course. The entity within me—Elizabeth—was still firmly caged in my mind. This last little outburst had been me. *All me.*

After a moment, Allison looked at me. There was sweat on her forehead. "What does it mean?"

"I don't know," I said.

"And you really don't care about the missing hikers?"

"I'm trying to," I said, then paused and looked away. "But some people deserve to die."

"I think I need to go, Sam."

I nodded. "I think you should, too."

24.

Good evening, Moon Dance.

When you say it that way, Fang, I wrote in my little IM window, *I always hear Bela Lugosi's Dracula.*

Maybe that's how I'd intended it to sound, Sam. What's on your mind?

My fingers briefly hovered over the keyboard before I typed: *How can I keep doing my job...if I no longer care?*

Care about what?

If people die?

His answer came a half minute later: *I'm not sure what to say to that, Moon Dance.*

But surely you agree, I wrote. *We are the same, you and I. We are hunters, are we not?*

We are, Sam. But we can decide who to hunt and what to hunt and when to hunt. Or to not hunt at all. You have a viable source of blood from a willing donor.

I shook my head there on my couch, although he couldn't see me shake it. The lights were out and, although it wasn't quite twilight yet, the room was dark enough. The sun had set about an hour ago and I was feeling...hungry. Allison had left before my feeding, and my body was letting me know it. My stomach never growled, nor did I feel hungry, as I remembered it back when I was mortal. No, this was different. This was a physical need. I suspected this is what a heroin addict felt—an overwhelming desire to satisfy the deepest yearning. To the point where rational thought went out the window.

I missed my feeding today, I wrote. *I think I was scaring her.*

You're scaring me, Sam. You have the cow and pig blood packets.

Fuck the packets.

I'm coming over. I have my own packets. Human blood. Are you home?

Yes.

Sit tight.

He logged off.

Except I didn't sit tight, whatever the hell that means. I closed my laptop and stood and paced my small room and wished like hell my living room was bigger so I could pace in longer steps. I didn't have to live this way. I could have more money. I could take the money I needed from those who had it. I could then take their lives, too. I could take and take and take, and nothing could stop me, not ever.

I paced the small room and shook my hands, then ran my fingers through my hair. I was hungry. *Starving.* I shouldn't have let her leave without first feeding from her. I had cow and pig blood in the garage, mixed with all sorts of filthy pollutants.

I deserved better than that.

I paused at my big living room window. It looked out from my end of the cul-de-sac, all the way down the street, itself lined with houses on either side. Most had big trees out front. Lots of cars were parked out front, too. It was evening. My kids were with my sister. I had begged her to take them. I wasn't feeling like myself...I'd told her. She had looked oddly at me when I had dropped them off.

Now, along the street, I saw some kids playing. A sort of chasing game as they weaved in and out of parked cars. Reckless. Careless. Shitty parenting. I watched the kids some more. Laughing and now playing a game of tag. Refreshing, actually. Still, why would you let your kids play outside when there were predators out there? Predators watching them, even now. Predators who would snatch their kids away.

Stupid fucking parents.

I paced in front of the window. I wondered what those same parents would think if they knew an honest-to-god vampire lived on their very street. Something that drank blood and stayed up at night and watched their children play.

I shook my head, rubbed my eyes and paced some more...and then, I saw it. The thing I had been hoping to see. It was exactly what I needed, but hadn't known, until now.

It was a tomcat, walking along the wall that separated my front yard from my neighbor's front yard.

Before I could think, before I could plan, I was out my front door, pouncing faster than I ever thought I could, and certainly faster than the cat had expected.

It was a short time later when I heard the familiar voice behind me. "Ah, shit, Sam."

I pushed the remains of the cat away, tossing aside a leg that I had been sucking the marrow out of.

"Aaron," I said, using Fang's assumed name. He was, after all, officially on the run and wanted for murder. "Fancy meeting you here."

25.

Fang spent the next half hour cleaning me up, and cleaning my place up, too.

He deposited what was left of the cat in a heavy trash bag, along with my clothes, which he had made me strip out of in the bathroom and pass through to him. I noted that he averted his eyes.

Rather chivalrous of him.

I also noted that I was still ravenously hungry. The cat hadn't been nearly enough, although it had, for now, satisfied my need to kill something.

My *overwhelming* need to kill something.

And when I had killed it, when I had held its broken body in my hands and tore into it with my mouth, I knew something inside of me had died...and might stay dead forever.

My humanity.

This was, I was certain, the first time I had killed something that didn't deserve to die, something that hadn't done anything to me. Something that was, in fact, innocent. The cat was not only dead...but I had torn it to shreds, even going so far as breaking apart its bones to get to the good stuff inside.

"This is not like you, Moon Dance," said Fang from my living room, where he was presently wiping up the bloody mess from the wood floor.

I was dressed in a bathrobe. The now-bloody rag he was using intrigued me. "I suppose not," I said, and sat down on one end of the couch and watched him.

"You always had so much self-control."

"I was weak then."

"No," said Fang. "You were yourself."

"Well, this is me now. Get used to it. Did you bring the blood?"

"It's in the refrigerator."

He had barely finished the sentence when I was moving, flashing across the room—and probably flashing him, too. I didn't care if I flashed him. I only cared about the blood.

Human blood.

From Fang's own blood bank.

And there it was, in a white paper bag. Heavy bag, too, full of life, full of my sweet addiction.

I pulled out the first clear packet. Fang had used plastic medical bags to store his blood, all very official looking. I bit through the corner, spitting out the plastic, and drank deeply from it. I noted immediately—all over again—the difference between human and animal blood.

So different, I thought. *So perfect. And so right for me. Clearly, the entity within me preferred human blood.*

No, I thought, *I preferred it.*

I started on the second.

"Easy, Tiger," said Fang.

I opened my eyes. Yeah, I think they might have rolled back into my head. Like a shark. No, like a predator. Fang was leaning a shoulder against the kitchen doorway, watching me with an expression of bewilderment, amusement and concern.

Pick an expression, asshole, I thought.

And as I drank, I sensed myself slipping a little further away. A little further offshore, so to speak. The tide of hate and anger and hunger was pulling me further out to sea.

"Penny for your thoughts," said Fang, which was almost funny, since the man had once read my thoughts with ease. Now, no more, being a fellow creature of the night.

I dropped the second bag on my kitchen floor, the remnants of which splattered over my bare feet and up onto the base of my refrigerator. Blood had also spilled onto my robe in my haste to suck down the packages.

I started on the third bag when it occurred to me that I'd killed my neighbor's cat, Tinker Bell.

It hadn't been a stray tomcat. It hadn't been wild. In fact, I had chewed through its collar in my haste to get to its neck, even spitting out the little jingle bell it wore. Something inside me had dehumanized it, so to speak. Had rendered it into nothing but a stray, when, in fact, it had been something: a loving house pet.

But what if, instead of Tinker Bell, one of my elderly neighbors had walked past? Would I have rendered one of them into nothing as well? Would I have convinced myself they were homeless? Or meth addicts? Or something beneath me? Would they, even now, be wrapped in a trash bag, rendered into shreds?

Or what if my kids had been home? Would I have dehumanized them, too? Would they even now be as dead as Tinker Bell?

The thought scared the unholy shit out of me, and I dropped to my knees and buried my face in my hands, and as I wept, I heard a voice not very deep inside my head—my own voice, in fact— whisper: "Pathetic."

26.

"Rough day, Moon Dance?"

"Shut up," I said, and tried to laugh but failed miserably. It sounded halfway between a cough and a sob.

We were sitting on my bed, with the shades pulled down, and drinking ice water. I couldn't stand the thought of more blood. I'd had my fill for tonight. For many nights.

"It's safe to say that you just saw me at my worst."

"Well, if that's your worst, Moon Dance, then I think we're going to be okay."

"No," I said. "You don't understand. Well, maybe you would understand. Actually, you would understand better than most."

"You're rambling, Sam."

"That's me," I said. "Ramblin' Sam."

"And what is it you think I don't understand?"

"It might have been only a cat—oh, God, Tinker Bell—but I seriously lost *all* control of myself."

"It was only a cat—not to say that Tinker Bell wasn't an awesome cat. So, try to relax. Deep breaths. You didn't kill anyone, right?"

I nodded, perhaps with a little less conviction than he wanted.

"Right?" he asked.

"Right," I said. "I didn't kill anyone. I swear."

"Pinky swear?"

"Yes, dammit. Just the cat, and I feel terrible enough as it is."

"Terrible is good, Sam."

"What do you mean?"

I had my down pillow laid over my lap. Fang was sitting opposite me, legs crossed as well. He was as tall as Kingsley, certainly, but not as big, not by a long shot. No one was. Perhaps ever. I doubted Kingsley could sit cross-legged on a bed to save his life. Having tree trunks for legs had that effect.

Speaking of Kingsley, I knew he would not be happy to know that Fang and I were currently sharing my bed. Of course, we were both sitting on my bed, and one of us was currently doubting her sanity, but guys tended to overlook such minor details. I had no reason to hide it from Kingsley, and I would tell him later, and he would just have to get over it. For now, Fang was the only vampire I knew, and certainly the only one I trusted.

"It's good that you feel terrible, Sam. We need you to feel terrible. That terrible part is your humanity."

"But it didn't feel terrible in the moment. It felt right. Damn right."

"I have no doubt, Sam."

Fang rested his elbows easily on his knees. He was a good-looking guy. Straight nose. Bright eyes. His pale complexion went without saying. Earlier in his transformation, he had gone to a dark place, and had stayed there for a while. During so, my relationship with Kingsley had blossomed all over again, and Fang and I had lost touch for many months. Our rebuilding was slow. A few emails. A few texts, and then the IM-ing started again. Officially, we were the last two people on earth to still instant message.

Anyway, I was glad he had pulled himself out of it. Mostly, I was glad to have my Fang back in my life again. Our relationship seemed to have evolved into a true friendship, which was what I needed. He seemed to be mostly okay with it.

Now, he studied me long and hard, and I knew he was wishing like crazy that he could dip into my thoughts again. He was my first, so to speak. My first telepathic link. And, as with all firsts, he held a special place in my heart.

"I think, Moon Dance, that the key here is to never allow yourself to get to that place again."

"What place?"

"That place of darkness. Hear me out. The Librarian told you that the key to defeat the thing within you—"

"And within you, too, I might add."

He nodded. "Yes, but so far, the thing within me has stayed buried deep, as had been the case with you."

He was right. Elizabeth had lain dormant for many years, only recently making an appearance... and making my life a living nightmare in the process.

Fang went on: "Anyway, the Librarian had told you that the key to defeating her was with love."

"He did, yes. Maybe he's the original hippie."

"Or maybe he knows what he's talking about," said Fang. "What if the love he's referring to is...love for *yourself*."

"I'm not following."

"Exactly," said Fang. "You have spent so long hating yourself for what you are. Hating yourself for what you have become. Hating the thing within you. Hating your predicament. Hating Danny. Hating anything that has come up against you—"

"And my nails."

I held up my hands. "I hate my nails."

"Right, your nails. Anyway, my point is this: your own self-hatred has awakened the beast within you. Literally. That is why, I think, she has made such a strong showing. You have created an environment within yourself for her to flourish."

"Hating myself is kinda my thing."

"I know, Sam. But you didn't do anything wrong. You don't deserve this. You deserve love. Self-love."

His words hung in the air, and I did my best to absorb them. Truthfully, the concept of loving myself seemed...foreign. Which shouldn't be the case. Not for me, not for anyone.

"Self-love," I said again, and for some reason, I giggled.

"Not that kind of self-love, Samantha Moon! But surely *that* wouldn't hurt either."

And, yeah, we both laughed...and, yeah, I'm pretty sure I would be keeping this last exchange from Kingsley. The big oaf didn't need to know everything, dammit. Of course, the poor guy was currently in lockdown mode at his residence. I was never, ever permitted to see him the day before the full moon or the day after. Which was fine by me. At this time of the month, he tended to be grumpy as hell anyway.

"You said something about never letting myself get to this point again. What did you mean by that?"

"You will need to be diligent in your feeding, Samantha. Get yourself on a regular schedule. Go back to the cow and pig blood, as filthy as it is."

"Wait, why?"

"Hear me out. It's filthy and disgusting, yes, but the key here is that you did not *crave* that blood. You did not hunger for it. You consumed it only to stay alive. However, you only awakened the beast within when you began consuming human blood on a regular basis."

"*She* prefers human blood," I said, nodding.

"Then don't give her what she wants."

"Don't feed the beast, you mean?"

"Right."

"But I need blood—"

"Of course you do. We both do. Our bodies have been forever altered by the entities within. But we don't need *human* blood. You don't need human blood. Cow and pig blood satisfy your cravings."

"But I'm not as strong—"

"Perhaps not. Or perhaps that's a false belief she's given you."

"I may not be able to go back—"

"You can, Sam. You have to. Or next time I come here..."

He didn't have to finish. We both knew what he meant. The next time he came here, he might not see a dead cat...but a dead person.

He said, "The key is love."

"And cow blood."

"Yes, Sam."

"So, how do you love yourself when you've hated yourself for so long?"

Fang reached over and took both my hands. He held my gaze for a long, long time, then finally shook his head. "Only you can answer that, Sam. But I think you might be better at it than you give yourself credit for."

27.

Fang was gone, and I was restless.

After much pacing and running my fingers through my hair, I decided it was time that I got real answers, and it was time that I started caring that real people might be getting killed in the worst way imaginable: being eaten alive.

Jesus.

With my kids now staying over with my sister—God bless her—I grabbed my car keys and hit the road.

***

I was parked in front of Gunther's house.

It was the middle of night, with dawn still hours

away. The street was quiet and Gunther's two-story home looked empty. I shouldn't have left his house this evening. I should have stayed here, watching it, then followed him. But I had let my hunger get the best of me, and now, he was gone. I was sure of it. After all, tomorrow was the full moon, and there was a very good chance Gunther was, even now, looking for his next victim.

Up in the San Bernardino Mountains, perhaps along a hiking trail.

Or, more likely, he was setting up on a carefully chosen trail. Come morning, he would wait for the perfect victim. He was fairly indiscriminate. Men and women alike...although he leaned toward women.

No, this wasn't a paying gig. I had no dog in this fight. And up until now, the idea of something hunting humans in the woods didn't seem entirely horrible.

It had seemed right. Natural.

The strong shall live, and all of that.

But now that my hunger had been satiated, and now that I had begun the process of removing the hate and anger from my thoughts...something interesting was happening.

Something Fang had predicted, that smart little bugger.

I started caring. I started feeling like my old self. I started realizing that killing the innocent wasn't right, no matter what, and if I could do something about it, then dammit, I would.

A simple shift in focus had been all that was needed.

A shift from hate to love.

"Self-love," I whispered and laughed lightly.

I needed to do something, and that something was to find his damn cabin in the woods. A cabin that was, I suspected, off the grid or owned by someone else. Or even owned by one of his victims.

So, I closed my eyes and projected my mind out.

A neat trick and one that every investigator should be so lucky to have the ability to do. Anyway, as my consciousness expanded, I focused on the house before me, and soon, I was pushing through the front door. My projected mind now stood in his foyer. From there, I scanned the house. Empty. Lights out, except for a single lamp near the camelback couch. The view before me flickered and wavered, like a TV going on the fritz. I was stretching my mental scanning abilities to the limit. I pushed on down the hallway, scanning into each room. The downstairs was empty. Back in the living room, I noticed a camera sitting on his mantel, pointed at the front door. It was the only such camera I saw. I also saw a home security system that seemed pretty elaborate. Motion detectors in all the living room corners.

I headed upstairs and confirmed the same, then took a quick peek in the garage. The Challenger was still here.

Someone picked him up, I realized, and returned

to my body.

I stepped out of my minivan...and slipped into the shadows around Gunther's home, searching for a way in. I ignored the downstairs windows; most would be wired. I continued around the house, reaching over and opening a side gate. No dog, but I knew that. I scanned the upper stories.

There, high up, was a circular vent that would lead, I assumed, into the attic. I would take my chances.

I leaped up onto the stone fence separating his property from his neighbor's. Now the neighbor might have a dog...but it turned out they didn't. Either way, I wasn't on the fence for long. From there, I gathered myself and sprang as high as I could. Turns out I can spring with the best of them. A moment later, I landed smoothly on the roof.

I dashed along the crest of the roof and leaped onto the second-story tiles. A moment later, using brute force, I had the attic vent off.

Once inside, I began removing my clothing.

All in a night's work.

28.

I was naked. In someone else's house.

Lucky for me, without clothing, the camera and motion sensors wouldn't pick me up. Still, I was naked. In someone else's house.

Feeling more than self-conscious, I headed down his stairs, careful not to touch anything. I might be undead and a supernatural badass, but I still left fingerprints.

The house was large, but not exceptionally so. I didn't see a basement entrance outside, nor did I expect there to be. Few homes in Southern California had basements. Anyway, the first floor consisted of a large living room with a black lacquer Steinway piano in one corner. The fireplace with its mantel and camera. The mantel had a few candles on it, which I thought was overkill. The living room was immaculate. Freshly vacuumed. Furniture polished. Magazines spread neatly over the coffee table. I looked but didn't see a copy of *The Werewolf Times* or *Furry Illustrated.*

I did see, however, an abundance of moon paraphernalia. What was the deal with that anyway? Okay, I get that their lives revolve around the damn thing, but did they also need to collect moon crap, too?

Apparently so.

Kingsley's office was adorned with the stuff, and so was Gunther's home. A full moon painting above the black leather camelback couch. A crescent moon painting over the piano. A supermoon photograph over the fireplace. Moon statues inside an inset glass display case. The statues ranged from the very elegant to the surreal to the absurd. A Dali-like moon, made of clay, in mid-dissolve, was seemingly spilling onto the glass shelf. Actually, I kinda liked that one.

I moved on.

The kitchen was behind the living room, around a central set of stairs that led to the upstairs bedrooms. The kitchen was modern and industrial and looked like it had never been used. There was, yes, a moon potholder hanging from a hook near the refrigerator. Moon magnets on the fridge. I was beginning to hate the moon. Which was sad, considering my cool last name.

So far, I hadn't set off any alarms.

I headed upstairs and into the master bedroom. Freshly cleaned and freshly vacuumed. Yes, Gunther had been busy tonight. Maybe he preferred coming home to a clean house after his monthly killings. Call it a quirk.

As I stood in his bedroom, hands on hips and leaving nothing to the imagination, I noted a distinct lack of *new* spirit energy. Sure, there were a couple of older energies, so old that they were barely recognizable as human. They ignored me completely, which most older energy did. No one had died here recently, I was certain of it. Gunther Kessler wasn't shitting where he eats, as the saying goes.

That's what the kill cabin was for.

I noted the motion detectors were reserved for downstairs, so I freely rummaged through drawers and closets upstairs. I checked pockets and inside shoes and behind dressers. I checked under his bed and under his mattress. I lifted paintings and flipped through books. No tell-tale receipts. No photographs. Other than being a closet E.L. James fan, he'd left no clues that I could discern. I next checked the guest room. Nothing.

I left the guest bedroom and headed down the short hall to his office, where I hoped to hit pay dirt. No such luck. Or dirt. The computers were password protected, and I barely remembered my own passwords. His filing cabinet would have been my best bet, except he didn't have one.

As I stood there in his office, naked as the day I

was born, feeling foolish and oddly liberated, I realized I only took Nancy Pearson's word for it that Gunther was a killer.

The truth was, outside of a ridiculous amount of moon paraphernalia, I wasn't even entirely sure the man was a werewolf. Even Kingsley hadn't known him. And Kingsley's wolfie friends weren't talking either.

Maybe Gunther had gone on a short trip. Maybe a taxi had picked him up. Or the airport shuttle. Or maybe he was hunting his next victim even now, in the woods, all while I stood naked in his house like an idiot.

I shouldn't have left the surveillance of his house.

But I had. I had let my hunger get the best of me.

It didn't have to be that way. I could have satiated it with a packet of animal blood. A cooler in the van, maybe. Fill it with a few emergency packets. I had convinced myself that I wanted—no, needed—human blood. Perhaps Fang was right. Perhaps that was a false belief. Perhaps giving *her* human blood only made her stronger, and me—the real me—weaker.

Most of all, she fed off my own self-hatred.

"No more," I thought.

Now, as I stood there in his office, hands on hips and thinking hard, I was certain of one thing: someone had picked him up. Whether it was a taxi or a shuttle or a fellow creature of the night, I didn't know.

But if I could figure out who picked him up...then I would find Gunther and his kill cabin in the woods.

29.

The call came the next morning.

These days, I tended to sleep lighter. Before, it would take a lot more than a phone call at 10 a.m. to wake me up. Especially after the night I'd had.

The phone number was restricted, which didn't surprise me. At least not on today, of all days.

The full moon.

It was all I could do to sound coherent, when I clicked on the call. "Moon Investigations," I said. At least, I think I said it.

"Rough night, Samantha?"

"Who's this?"

"Ranger Ted with the California State Parks."

It took a moment for that information to sink in. I was still lying on my side in bed, with my pillow mostly over my head.

"Got a minute?"

I sat up and yawned. "Sure, what's going on?"

"We have another hiker missing."

"Shit."

"You can say that again. You mentioned you met Sheriff Stanley the other day, right?"

"I did," I said, and nearly added that I'd helped save his marriage, but decided that might come off as unprofessional and a little egocentric...and a little off-topic. "Is he overseeing the case?"

"You could say that," said Ranger Ted. "It's his wife, Elise, who's missing."

"No," I said, and might have shouted it and sat a little straighter. "No, no, no."

I had seen the unborn children. I had felt his love for this woman. I had helped save the marriage, off-topic or not.

"Exactly. This isn't good, Sam. Not good at all. People know the two of them have been fighting. People even know that she cheated on him. We live in a small town. People talk. Speaking of which, there's already whispers that there might be foul play."

"Foul play, how?"

"Sheriff Stanley has a temper. He's been reprimanded in the past."

"No way," I said. "He would never have touched his wife. Not like that."

"And you know this how?"

"Just trust me on that."

"I wish I could, Sam. Either way, this doesn't look good for him, and it's looking worse and worse for her."

"When did she go missing?"

"This morning. She went on an early hike. At daybreak. She's usually home for breakfast at 7:30 at the latest."

I checked the time again. 10:10 a.m. "She's been missing for a little over two and a half hours," I said. "That's hardly a reason—"

"You don't understand, Sam. This is a small community. She told her husband she would be back in an hour. The word is out that Elise Stanley is missing. If someone had seen her, they would have reported her. I don't have a good feeling about this, Sam."

Neither did I. Try as I might to play devil's advocate, I knew full well that there might very well be a missing hiker today. Damn well. After all, Gunther was gone and tonight was the full moon.

"We have all available manpower on the case. We've even called in some boys from San Diego and Los Angeles counties. It's a sheriff's wife, after all. One of our own, in a way. Anyway, I thought you should have a heads up, since you were just here asking about missing hikers."

"Thank you," I said, and we clicked off. For the next few minutes, I thought about Sheriff Stanley and his three unborn children.

I got dressed, grabbed my keys, and hit the road.

30.

"Master Kingsley is terribly indisposed—"

"I'm terribly sorry to hear that," I said, and pushed past the tall butler and into the house.

He caught up behind me. Not hard for him to do with those long legs of his. His mismatched long legs, I might add. "Master Kingsley has given me strict orders—"

"I'm sure he did."

I was through Kingsley's big house and in his kitchen, and over to a nondescript side door that led, I knew, to his basement of horrors.

"I'm afraid I can't let you go down there—"

He had tried to bar the door down into the basement. Tried being the operative word here. I pulled it open, even while he had pressed it shut. I sensed that Franklin wasn't using all of his great strength. I also sensed that, despite perhaps not liking me very much—for reasons I still didn't understand—he would never use all of his strength against me. I sensed his restraint. Smart man.

Now, as I headed down the narrow flight of stone stairs, I might as well have been a half a world away, heading down into the dungeon of a forgotten castle along a mist-shrouded hillside. Dracula's castle.

"Master Kingsley will not be happy," said Franklin, following behind.

"Master Kingsley can bite me."

"No truer words have been spoken, I'm afraid."

I was about to reply when I paused in mid-step. I paused because something deep and rumbling seemed to emanate up through the stone steps themselves. Hell penetrated through the surrounding walls and ceiling.

"What the devil was that?"

"Again, no truer words have been spoken."

On that ominous note, I continued down the dimly lit stairs. As I neared the landing, a hand fell onto my shoulder. "Madam, please. Kingsley will not want you to see him like this. Please stop."

I stopped in mid-step and looked back. Franklin's pale face hovered in the darkness. Gone was his usual look of distaste for me. Why the man didn't like me, I may never know.

"Has he turned?" I asked.

Franklin shook his head. As he did so, I could

see the scars that stitched his right ear on. The stitching wasn't done with very much care. "It's still early, but the process has begun."

"Because it's a full moon somewhere," I said.

"Perhaps. You must turn back. I must insist on this."

"I know you're just doing your job, but so am I."

Strange energy flitted in the hallway below. Small, amorphous energy. Animal energy, I realized. Lots of it. The place might as well have been a slaughterhouse.

Lots of killing in here, I thought.

I had a vague idea what I was in for. I had, in fact, seen Kingsley completely transformed a few years ago. It was then that I had been introduced to the entity within him...and the realization that something was, in fact, in me as well.

"Please, *Sam*," said Franklin, and it was, I was certain, the first time he had used my first name. "I beg you. This will not be pretty."

"I'm not here for pretty," I said. "I'm here for help."

And with that, I turned my back on Franklin and continued down.

31.

I found myself in a narrow corridor, with a stone wall to the left, and a long metal wall to my right. I could have been walking along the hull of a great battleship. Halogen lighting flickered overhead, giving the impression of torchlight. You'd think Kingsley, with all of his bucks, would dish out some of it for better lighting.

Somewhere, water dripped.

And since we weren't anywhere near a Scottish loch, or under a medieval moat, I could only assume that Kingsley's sprinkler system was on the fritz.

No, I had never been down here before. But not for a lack of trying. Kingsley had been firm about keeping me away. Even to the point of being kind of a dick.

I heard Franklin stop behind me, felt him watching me, felt his disapproval, his concern.

I continued forward.

Before me, set into the steel wall, was a heavy-looking metal door that looked like it belonged on the space shuttle. As I walked, I heard...something on the other side of the metal wall. Breathing, perhaps.

As I continued, something thudded loudly on the other side of the wall, so loudly that the ground beneath me shook. I stopped and swallowed. Maybe this wasn't a good idea. Maybe I really didn't want to see Kingsley like this.

No, I thought. I had to talk with him...and now. A talk he and I had never had before, but it was time.

Another thud from the other side of the wall. This one louder, sounding as if something meaty and big had been slammed against the wall. There was only one thing meaty and big on the other side of that wall. That thing happened to be Orange County's most prominent defense attorney...

And my boyfriend.

Still another thunderous slam, and now, the wall next to me shook as well. Dust sifted down from above, and the light flickered, went out briefly, and then flickered back on again. I continued down the cement corridor.

The closer I got to the metal door, the more I could smell it: death.

Putrid death, too.

Something that been dead for many, many days. Perhaps even a week.

I looked back and saw Franklin staring out at me from the shadows of the stairway. I was beginning to understand why they had tried so hard to keep me away...

The entity within me perked up at the smell, but I had been doing a pretty damned good job of keeping her locked up, so I wrapped a few more mental iron bars around the cage I imagined her in.

A few years ago, I would have gagged at the smell of death. Now, not so much. Now, I was intrigued by it. What had died? How had it died? Perhaps I could never truly go back to who I had been. Perhaps I'd done too many things, seen too many things.

Still, I tried to find a neutral feeling about the smell. In fact, I tried to not have any feeling about the smell at all. My new goal these days was to not give the entity within me any hope. Or any escape.

With each step I took, the pounding on the other side of the wall seemed to keep pace with me, but as I reached the door, the sound stopped altogether, and a deathly silence followed.

More nervous than I thought I would be, I stood just to the side of the door. There was a small, square opening in the door, no bigger than a small fist. Certainly not big enough for Kingsley to reach through. Most important, I could see that the door itself was at least six inches thick.

Jesus.

Now, from the other side of the door, I heard the breathing. Deep and ragged. Something was just off to the side of the door, listening to me. That something was, of course, Kingsley.

At least, I hoped it was.

I held my breath; after all, the putrid stench was pouring through the opening in the door. Muted light came through, too. The light was high up, casting a squarish light on the floor before me.

"Kingsley," I said hesitantly. "It's Sam—"

A face suddenly appeared in the small opening. A very hairy and sweating face...wild and contorted and in obvious pain. I squeaked and took a step back.

"Sam!" Kingsley gasped, pressing his face into the square opening. "What...what are you doing here?"

Now that I saw him like this—desperate, wild, angry, shocked, and in mid-transformation—I wanted to *un*see it. I also wanted to *un*smell what I was smelling. Maybe this was a bad idea.

But it wasn't. I needed him. I needed help.

"I...I have to speak to you—"

"Leave, Sam!" he growled, and turned away from the square, I could see him pacing through the opening, passing back and forth behind it. God, he looked massive, the few glimpses I saw.

"I'm sorry, Kingsley, but I can't."

"I'm warning you, Sam..."

He wasn't himself. I could see that. Or, rather, he was tapping into a very, very angry and primal and hate-filled part of him.

The demon, I thought. *It's the demon coming through.*

I powered on, "How do I stop a werewolf?"

I knew all the stories. I'd heard all the rumors. The truth was, I really didn't know. It wasn't a question I'd ever needed to ask Kingsley. I suspected Fang would know the answer. But I didn't feed into rumors or legends. I needed to know facts, and I needed to stop Gunther tonight.

"Why, Sam?" he growled, pacing behind the small opening, each footfall shaking the ground beneath me. If I had to guess, I would guess that he was easily a foot taller, and maybe another hundred pounds heavier.

And he would only get bigger.

And stronger.

"Gunther has another hiker. A woman this time. A woman I know, well, kind of, long story—"

"Enough!" he roared, and I shrank back. And it took a godawful lot to get me to shrink back. But never, never had I heard such force and powerful volume from a human.

Because he isn't human, I thought. *At least, not now.*

I knew Kingsley could transform into a wolf—as in an actual wolf—at will. Few werewolves had this ability to shapeshift. But on the night of the full moon, he didn't turn into a wolf. No, he turned into a hulking, hybrid monster. A true wolfman.

We were still hours from dusk and already he'd

changed so much. I knew his transformation was a slow, painful process for him. Unlike the wolf that he could conjure quickly—which, I suspected, was closer to what I did with the winged Talos—his monthly transformation into a hulking beast was nearly unbearable for him. After all, this was when the entity within made a full appearance and, while doing so, apparently delighted in torturing Kingsley along the way.

"I don't care about the hiker, Sam..." His voice rattled, rumbled, like an idling Harley.

"You do, Kingsley," I said. I almost said 'Wolfie,' which was my term of endearment for him, although he didn't much like it...unless, of course, we were in his bedroom.

He yanked his head away from the square opening and stretched his neck to and fro, and I saw what was happening. His neck was getting bigger. Muscle mass was appearing before my eyes. Muscle mass and fur. He grunted and might have whimpered.

"Leave, Sam. Leave, goddammit."

This wasn't the Kingsley I knew. The man I knew was attentive and playful, even if a little stubborn. This creature, stalking behind the door, was only a semblance of the man I now loved. The immortal I loved.

"Kingsley, please—"

He growled as he paced behind the door. I could only see flashes of him behind the small window. The flashes that I saw were horrific at best. With each passing minute, I would lose more and more of him. I doggedly asked my question.

"How do I stop a werewolf, Kingsley?"

I saw him shaking his head as he paced. "Too strong," he was saying, mumbling. "Too strong, even for you."

I wasn't so sure about that, but I wasn't going to argue the point.

Kingsley went on: "Kill and destroy and feed, and will fight to the death once engaged."

"Then tell me how to defeat him, Kingsley."

"Don't do it, Sam. Wait...for me."

"He has to be stopped. Tonight."

He didn't like my answer and pulled away angrily. His heavy footfalls seemed heavier than just a few minutes earlier. His great head and beefy shoulders appeared and disappeared through the square opening.

Now, I pressed my face into the square opening. "Tell me, Kingsley. Tell me what you know."

I sensed his hesitation. After all, once I knew how to defeat a werewolf, I would know how to defeat him, too. A small, protective side of him was keeping that information from me. Or not. But that was my guess.

Suddenly, Kingsley's thick, sweating, panting face appeared just inches from mine. I saw the fangs pushing through his gums, which bled profusely. It was only noon and he was suffering so much. I had no idea he went through such a prolonged, hellish transformation. And he still had many hours to go.

How many hours, exactly, I didn't know. When did a werewolf turn into a full-blown werewolf? At sunset? At dusk? At midnight? At the first sign of the full moon? I didn't know exactly. But looking at Kingsley now, it looked like the transformation wasn't very far away.

And I still had to find Gunther.

Shit...

"We are not so different, Sam," he said, gasping. Blood bubbled between his lips. "The same silver that kills you, kills me."

"A silver dagger—"

"No, Sam. You'll never get close enough with a dagger. He'll be too fast, too powerful. You've never seen anything like this, Sam."

"Then what?"

"A silver bullet."

"But where..."

"Franklin..." he gasped. "Franklin has them. Just in case..."

He held my gaze, although his bloodshot eyes wavered. I got his meaning: just in case he ever got out and needed to be put down. Of course, he had gotten out a few years ago. Where was Franklin then? A question for another time.

"Go, Sam! Leave me be!"

With that, he slammed his huge hands against the door, and kept slamming them until I gulped and skittered off down the hallway, back to where Franklin was still waiting in the shadows. The thick, metal wall vibrated. More dust and dirt sifted down.

***

Upstairs in the oversized kitchen, as Franklin locked the door that led down into the cellar, I said, "That smell..."

"A deer carcass," said Franklin, turning to look down at me as he pocketed the key. "I hunted it last week."

I nodded, sickened and relieved...relieved that it wasn't a human corpse. Sickened that I kiss that mouth of his. "And it's been rotting down here ever since, I presume."

"You presume correctly. Master Kingsley prefers them...putrid. The more putrid, the better."

I felt my stomach turn, which in itself was a good sign for me. It meant that I was keeping the bitch at bay. The crazy, crazy bitch. Far below, the earth shook violently, as did the kitchen walls around us.

"When will Kingsley fully turn?"

"At sundown, of course," said Franklin. "Like all true creatures of the night."

I almost asked what kind of creature he was...except I thought I just might know. Not so much a creature as a *creation*.

I had six hours, at most. Five, if I wanted to play it safe.

"I need those silver bullets, Franklin."

He looked at me long and hard, then nodded. "This way, Ms. Moon."

32.

I was sitting in my minivan, along Kingsley's crushed-shell driveway, weeping.

To think that my boyfriend would be feasting on something dead and rotting...in just a few hours...was a little upsetting.

I shouldn't have seen him. Perhaps Franklin would have told me how to stop a werewolf. Or perhaps not. His loyalty to Kingsley ran deep...and for reasons I didn't quite understand. Yes, I had suspected it would be silver. The same silver that removed the entity from me would remove it from him, too.

Except, I would have gone into the fight with a silver dagger, and I might not have returned. Yes, I had known a werewolf would be powerful...but I hadn't quite grasped just how powerful. The silver bullet was the key, of course.

And not getting too close.

I looked at the Smith & Wesson .357 Magnum sitting on the seat next to me, chambered with the six silver bullets.

It would take a helluva shot. Especially at a charging werewolf.

I was risking my life, I knew. I was risking everything that I held dear. I was risking, most of all, being a mother to my children. No, I didn't think a werewolf needed to use silver to kill me. Ripping me from limb to limb, and then devouring me, would probably do the job, too.

I looked at Kingsley's sprawling estate before me. I was certain I could hear his roars from here, and feel a slight rumbling beneath me. He was angry. He was turning. What happened to him each month wasn't very fair either.

I wiped my eyes and considered my next move. I had to find Gunther, of course. He was up there, in the woods, changing throughout the day, much like Kingsley was. And nearby was a woman. A live woman. Waiting to be consumed by him, no doubt watching his transformation in complete and utter horror.

Some preferred them dead and rotted, others preferred them fresh and alive. I was happy to see that I remained repulsed by both notions.

I drummed my fingernails on the steering wheel, knowing my time was slipping through, well, these very fingers.

On a whim, I pulled out my cell phone and typed in "cars and mustaches."

What came up next was very intriguing.

Very, very intriguing.

33.

I was back in the city of Orange, parked this time in Gunther's driveway.

He wouldn't be using it anytime soon. After all, I had no doubt he was in the midst of a full-blown transformation. And in the company of one woman —the wife of my new friend, Sheriff Stanley—who was, no doubt, witnessing all of it. Then again, if this script played out, she would be doing far more than witnessing. She would be an unwilling participant.

So, I did what any normal investigator would do under the circumstances: I downloaded an app to my iPhone, the Lyft app to be precise. An app that was, in fact, pure genius.

According to the website, with a simple touch of

a button, the Lyft driver closest in proximity to me (thanks to my phone's GPS) would get pinged that I needed a ride. The app also connected our Facebook pages, apparently for safety reasons. My Facebook page sported an outdated picture of me from nine years ago, back when I was camera-friendly. Luckily, I didn't look much different now.

Which wasn't a good thing, I suspected. Soon, I would be getting to the point where my friends and colleagues were clearly looking older than me...by nearly a decade.

Worry about that later, I thought, when the app had finished downloading.

I was almost giddy with excitement.

When the app opened, I pressed the "pick me up" button and waited. While I waited, I sweated. The day was sweltering. I might be immortal but I got hot—and sweated—with the best of them. Which is why I had the A/C running in the minivan while I waited.

A moment later, my phone chirped.

A driver had locked onto me and was en route. Okay, now I was definitely giddy. In fact, there he was on Facebook. A youngish-looking Latino with a round face and wide-set eyes. I scanned Paulo's profile because I had nothing better to do. Married. A writer on the side. I checked out the links to his books, too. A vampire series, of all things. A witch series, too. And something about gods in Los Angeles.

"This should be interesting," I said.

According to the app, he was only two minutes away. I looked at the time on my cell: 1:38. According to my weather app, sunset was at 6:19 p.m.

I did some serviceable math. I had five-and-a-half hours before a woman would be consumed alive by a real werewolf.

And, yeah, I cared, dammit. I cared a lot. I had met her husband. I had met her unborn kids. They needed her, dammit. They needed her alive. They had a family to build. Not to mention, I had given Sheriff Stanley some of my best marital advice. I didn't want to see that advice go down the drain.

Not funny, I know. But try as I might, my new morbid sense of humor didn't seem to be going anywhere.

"Choose your battles," I said to myself.

After all, a morbid sense of humor I could live with. Not giving a shit about death—and feasting on my neighbor's cat because I couldn't control myself —wasn't something I could live with.

Quite frankly, I was better than that. I lived to fight the bad guys. I lived to protect the innocent. I was not a bad guy myself. I was one of the good ones, dammit, and I was going to do everything I could think of to ensure just that.

That I stayed as good as possible.

Further down the block, a white Toyota Prius turned onto the street. As it approached, I could see the driver through the windshield, sort of leaning forward, forearms wrapped around the steering wheel, scanning. Yup, it was the same guy in the Facebook page—Paulo, the vampire/witch/demigod writer. Most telling was the furry mustache attached to the front grill of the Prius. My Lyft ride had appeared.

I stepped out of my minivan, waving. He frowned, thick eyebrows bunching up, then pulled into the driveway, next to my minivan. He jumped out, smiling, but also looking confused as hell.

"I'm sorry," he said, talking fast, eyes scanning somewhat wildly. He either had a serious case of A.D.D., or something else was going on. "But I'm a little confused. You need a ride, right?"

"Maybe. Mostly, I need some information."

"Okay, now I'm a lot confused." Paulo gave me an easy laugh, although his eyes never stopped scanning.

A.D.D., I thought. *And bad.*

"First," I said, "why are you confused?"

"Because I usually pick up Gunther at this address."

"Only Gunther?"

"Yes. What's going on here? Do you need a ride or—"

I stepped forward and reached out to his mind. Holy sweet hell, that was a scrambled, nearly incoherent mind. I reached deeper, through the chaotic miasma of thought streams, and found his core and told him to relax and to answer my questions, and that I was a friend.

He nodded, and for the first time, his eyes

settled down, and settled on me. He exhaled. I suspected this was the first break his mind had had in years. Decades, perhaps.

"First question," I said. "Why do so many Lyft cars come down this street?"

"It's because Gunther tips so well. Usually $200."

"But I thought the app summoned drivers, not the other way around."

He nodded, smiling easily. He was good-looking, in a round-faced, wide-eyed sort of way. "It does work that way, in theory. But some Lyft drivers will game the system. After all, the system pings the closest driver, so we'll sometimes patrol areas where known big tippers live or work, hoping to get pinged. With Gunther, we know we can make an easy $200, especially when it starts getting close to the full moon."

I blinked. "What do you know about the full moon?"

The driver shrugged, still looking at me, eyelids dropping a little. Now that his rapidly-running mind had shut off, he was getting sleepy.

"We Lyft drivers sort of figured it out, since he'd been doing this for so long."

"Doing what for so long?"

"Grabbing a lift up to Big Bear. Turns out, it's every full moon."

"Has he told you why he leaves every full moon?"

"He told me he's an amateur astronomer. That

he has a cabin in the woods where he has a tele-scope."

My heart thumped once, twice, loudly, excitedly.

"And why does he tip so much?"

Here, the Latino driver paused and fought against my control, but I silently encouraged him to continue and he finally nodded. "He pays us to keep quiet about the location."

"Have you seen the cabin?"

"No, but I drop him off at the same spot every time."

"Why don't you take him to the cabin?"

"I dunno. I just do what he says."

"Did you take him this last time?"

"No, but I kinda hoped I hadn't missed him."

"Which was why you were patrolling nearby," I said.

"Right."

"When do you usually take him up to the cabin?"

"Usually two days before, sometimes three."

"Will you take me to the cabin, too?"

His eyes flicked over me and he smiled. "Of course, Samantha Moon."

"And after you take me to the woods, I want you to forget we had this conversation."

He gave me an easy smile. "I'll do my best."

And with that, I slipped into the front passenger seat of the Prius and we were off.

34.

I checked the time: just past 2 p.m.

Sunset was in four hours, and it was a two-hour drive up to Big Bear, which was higher and further back than Arrowhead. I thought about that as we drove, then nodded. Yes, Gunther kidnapped them in Arrowhead...and then brought them back to Big Bear.

He has a vehicle up there, I thought.

Why he left his car in Orange County, I didn't know. I suspected it was an attempt to cover his tracks. Of course, the Lyft drivers themselves might start getting suspicious. I had a thought.

"Are you aware of any Lyft drivers disappearing?"

Paulo was still feeling the effects of my earlier

mental prompting, and so he answered easily enough. "Two of them over the past few months, actually. Both were found killed in their cars. Both in Orange County. There's a running joke that being a Lyft driver in Orange is the new most dangerous job."

I nodded. The bastard was covering his tracks there, too.

As my own Lyft ride commenced, he drove through Orange and headed for the 22 Freeway. I imagined Gunther standing on, say, a boulder, overlooking a popular—or perhaps not-so-popular —hiking trail, and hunting his next target.

Perhaps he used a tranquilizer gun. Or perhaps he used a real gun, and shot them in, say, the foot. Or perhaps he ambushed them or trapped them or lured them into his car.

I didn't know, and it wasn't important how he found them. Since none had survived, I might never know. What mattered was stopping him from preying on the innocent. From killing tonight.

And ever again.

My own entity, of course, would prefer me to kill and maim and torture and to control. And, if I gave her half a chance, she would possess me fully and do it for me.

It did take some fortitude to take on these entities, to fight against them...and to not give in.

Had Kingsley given in? Was he weak by allowing the thing within him to feast on the rotted deer carcass? Maybe, maybe not. I didn't know just how far Kingsley had let the entity out. Maybe they had come to some agreement: if Kingsley feeds it what it most wants, perhaps it lets him live a normal enough life. Not feasting on a human corpse was, perhaps, Kingsley drawing the line. *Maybe.*

I didn't know, but what I did know was this: there would be no agreement between myself and Elizabeth, the woman inside me, the woman who fueled me, the highly evolved dark master...and perhaps the highest evolved of them all.

No compromise. No getting out, ever.

The bitch picked the wrong person.

Moving on. Admittedly, I was nervous as hell to confront Gunther, even if he was half the size of Kingsley. Either way, he was going to be trouble. Perhaps more trouble than I was ready for. I patted my purse next to me, which concealed the Smith & Wesson. This gave me some comfort. Not much, but enough.

I considered calling Allison for backup. She might be needy as hell sometimes—even dingy—but man, oh man, was that girl a force to be reckoned with.

Still, I thought, chewing my lip as we eased onto the freeway, there was no way in hell I was going to expose her to the ferociousness of a werewolf. No, she was out. Fang could be of help—a lot of help. I pulled out my phone and clicked on the messenger and nearly sent him a text.

No, I thought. He would be weak all the way up to sundown. Truth was, I was weak, too, although not as weak as before, back when I didn't own the ring. I was operating, I suspected, at about eighty percent, which wasn't that bad. The problem being, of course, when I got to full strength at sundown, Gunther would be fully turned, too. And he would be at full strength, as well.

And a full-blown werewolf.

Another thing: I was feeling a tad guilty about my time with Fang the other night. Yes, he had talked me down and given me the world's best advice on how to beat the thing within me, but I was still feeling some guilt about us in my bedroom, holding hands.

I would tell Kingsley about it. He would understand. I hoped.

With all of that settled in my mind, I planned to get to Big Bear well before Gunther turned. Of course, I still had to find his kill cabin, which I highly doubted doubled as an observatory, as purported.

So, I settled back for the two-hour drive, mentally going through how I would face a partially-turned werewolf, when my phone rang.

Restricted number. These days, that was never a good sign.

"Moon Investigations," I said.

"Sam, it's Sherbet."

"Do you always refer to yourself by your last name, Detective?"

"Almost always. We have your daughter."

I sat up. "What do you mean?"

"We found her in the park, drunk as a skunk. You need to come get her."

35.

I had Paulo alter our course and we headed out to Fullerton along the 57 Freeway.

Now, with the Lyft driver waiting for me outside—I might have compelled him to wait for me, I didn't, after all, want to lose him—I found my daughter in Sherbet's office, sitting before his desk with her head buried in her arms, as a female officer stroked her hair. Sherbet himself sat back in his desk and didn't look too happy. Then again, I couldn't remember the last time Detective Sherbet looked too happy.

"We found her in Hillcrest Park, drinking with her buddies."

"Who found her?"

"One of our boys. We got a report of some kids

drinking and smoking and making general asses of themselves. Turned out to be true. The others scattered like frightened fish. This one tried to scatter. Turned out she was too drunk to scatter, and instead, fell flat on her face. Don't worry, she's okay. Just a few scrapes."

Tammy moaned, her face still buried in her arms.

I thanked the female officer, who gave Tammy a final pat, and gave me a consoling smile, then got up and left. I had a distinct impression that the officer had been there before, with her own kids.

I took the seat next to my daughter, except I very much didn't feel like stroking her head. It was all I could do to not chew her ass out. I took a few deep breaths.

Easy, Sam, came Sherbet's telepathic words.

I'm too pissed off to be easy about anything, I shot back, *and she can hear you, so be careful.*

He nodded, then said aloud, "Should have figured."

"Is she still drunk?" I asked.

"My guess: yes. We probably should have had her checked out at St. Jude's." He shrugged. "She didn't look sick and responded well enough."

"Can you leave us alone?" I asked him.

"You do realize that I'm a busy homicide investigator, right? And the *busy* part isn't necessarily a good thing."

Please, I thought to him.

He sighed and his cop mustache fluttered a

little. Then he hefted his thickish body from behind the desk and made his way toward the door.

"Thickish?" he said.

"You know what I meant," I said.

He might have sighed again, and then left us alone, shutting his office door behind him.

36.

I checked the time...2:30. Less than four hours.

"Less than four hours for what, Mom?" asked Tammy, her face still buried in her arms.

"Never mind that," I said, and threw up a mental wall about all things wolfish.

"You're hiding something, Mo—"

"Never mind what I'm hiding, young lady. Do you care to explain yourself?"

"No. And quit shouting. My head..."

The stench of beer wafted from her as well as the blood from the scrapes on her face. Like a shark, I can smell fresh blood within a few dozen feet. Not always a good thing, especially in a room full of women.

"Gross, Mom," said Tammy, obviously following my thoughts.

"Don't change the subject, young lady."

"Hey, you're the one talking about—"

"Never mind that, Tamara Moon," I said, using her full name, which meant that I meant business.

Instead, she giggled. "Relax, Mom. Sheesh. Everyone drinks a little—"

I moved her chair around to face me, dragging it easily with one hand over the carpet. Tammy, whose head had been propped up on the desk, pitched forward, "Hey!"

"Don't 'hey' me, and look at me when I'm talking to you."

She did, and for the first time, I saw her bloodshot eyes and puffy lower lip. I stood and paced in Sherbet's office, glancing at the clock overhead. 2:45. I didn't have time for this...and yet, I had to make the time.

"How long have you been drinking?"

She shrugged. "A few months now."

"Where do you get the alcohol?"

"Friends. Friends of friends. Mostly we steal it from—"

I spun around and nearly yanked her to her feet...at a police station, no less. Inside a clear glass office, no less. Sherbet, who was talking on his cell phone in a nearby cubicle, raised a hand and lowered it, motioning for me to calm down. Good advice.

"Relax, Mom. Sheesh. We didn't steal from stores. Just from parents, mostly."

"Have you stolen from me?"

She looked away, "Maybe a bottle..."

"Tammy!"

"...or two," she finished.

I sat again and ran my fingers through my hair and knew I was making a scene. I had to calm down about this. Then again, I'd never faced anything like this before—whatever *this* was. Teenage rebellion? Jesus, she was *barely* a teen. If this was a taste of what I was in for...well, I was in trouble.

"Relax, Mom—"

"You tell me to relax again, and so help me God, I will bend you over my knee right here—"

"No, you won't. You would never embarrass Sherbet like that...and risk going to jail, even though I don't think any jail could hold you."

"Don't talk back to me, young lady. And don't tell me what I will and won't do."

"Okay, sorry, geez."

"And don't 'geez' me."

"Okay, I won't geez you," she said, and broke into a grin, and for some damn reason, I broke into a grin, too. She knew she had me, and she knew how to push, too. "Who would ever want to *geez* you anyway."

I laughed, and said, "Okay, stop. Now I'm looking really bad."

"It's no big deal, Mom. Everyone does it, and I like to do it. It's fun to drink. I know why Auntie and you like to drink now, and all the adults in all of the commercials. It makes sense—"

"Just stop," I said, holding my head and resuming my pacing. I looked at the time: 2:52. "How do you feel?"

"Buzzed."

To hear my little girl tell me she felt "buzzed" was enough to drive *me* to drink. "We're going to talk about this later. Get your stuff, let's go."

And we went, this time detouring toward my sister's house in Placentia, which was next door to Fullerton. My sister was gonna be thrilled to see us. I texted her brief details and she texted back her confirmation to bring Tammy. Gotta love Mary Lou. She was my right-hand woman.

Meanwhile, my daughter slept it off, while Paulo, our Lyft driver, drove steadily, sometimes casting sideways glances my way, and in the rearview mirror at my daughter snoozing in the back seat.

We dropped off Tammy with a stern Mary Lou and then continued toward the original destination.

I checked the time: an hour wasted.

37.

"This is it," said Paulo.

"This is where you drop off Gunther?"

"Yup."

"Every time?"

"Yup."

"And is this where the others drop him off, too?"

"I wouldn't know that."

I briefly scanned Paulo's thoughts and took a look at his aura. He was telling the truth. We were parked on a side road that had ended as soon as it began. Massive cement blocks, connected with thick cables, barred the way further. The drive had been speedy enough. We had, in fact, made decent time. I checked my cell.

5:20.

I had just over an hour to find his cabin, find him, stop him, and save Elise Stanley.

All in a day's work, I thought, then turned to my driver. I commanded him to forget me, forget our conversation and forget about this tip. He would, I knew, still get paid for his efforts, even if he didn't remember his efforts. My account would be charged for the trip, so he would at least get something out of this, even if it was a big hole in his memory.

When he was gone, I found myself alone at the end of the blockaded street.

We had very much gone off the beaten path. Indeed, we had taken at least a half-dozen roads to get to this one. In fact, the two roads before this road had both been dirt, including this one.

Few, if anyone, would have known about this spot.

I checked the sun, and knew instinctively it was about an hour before it set. The day was still warm, but I was wearing jeans and a gray tank top. I let some air in the tank top, and kind of wished I could let some air in the jeans, too, but decided that would be unseemly, even for me.

Additionally, I was not at full strength, but neither was I shrinking away from the sun. I felt, in fact, pretty damn good. In about an hour, I would feel pretty damn great.

I doubted Gunther—or Kingsley—would feel pretty damn great in an hour. I suspected they sort of lost their minds for a while, or shrank so far into the background that they might as well have been frightened children hiding in a closet from their abusive parents.

The air was infused with pine and juniper, scents I love. A small wind moved some of the branches overhead, where birds tweeted continuously, apparently unaware of the 140-character limit.

I wasn't what you would call an outdoorsman or a master tracker, but I could see footprints in the dirt with the best of them. And I saw them now. Boot prints. Men's boots. How old, I didn't know, but my guess was within the past few days.

I didn't see another print, and certainly not a female's. Which suggested that this was only Gunther's Lyft drop-off point. From here, he hiked. To where, I didn't know. But to another vehicle, I suspected. And, of course, to a kill cabin.

With the sun now slipping behind the massive evergreens, I stepped over the cable barring the dirt road...and followed the prints.

At some point, I started jogging lightly, easily.

Not too much further, the footprints ended in a field of grass and I lost his trail. I looked for any telltale signs of beaten-down grass or a trail that might have picked up elsewhere. I didn't find it.

The wind was blowing stronger now, flattening the grass. I spied the full moon above, creeping up from the distant horizon. It was getting darker, and I was losing hope, until I realized I had, of course, an ace up my sleeve.

Speaking of sleeves, I disrobed, bundled up my clothing, and summoned the single flame.

38.

I was flying.

I also wasn't too worried about being caught. After all, I was in a very remote part of the mountains, and the day was losing light rapidly, too rapidly for my taste.

Was there really a woman being held against her will, waiting to be feasted on? Even now, was she perhaps watching a man stalk and pace before her, slowly shape-changing throughout the day, and now, undoubtedly, much faster?

Hard to believe...but it was all adding up.

I didn't need to know that I was down to the last twenty minutes. Hell, from up here and above the trees, I could see the sun slipping away to the west.

My clothing hung in a bundle below me on my

talons, all stuffed into my purse, along with the gun and silver bullets.

I ranged far and wide, buffeted by wind, sometimes sailing, sometimes flapping hard. All while I searched with eyes that were a lot better than my own. From up here, I saw trash on the ground. I even saw mice scurrying. I saw rabbits and lizards, all while flying hundreds of feet above.

Still, I was losing hope.

Maybe Sheriff Stanley's wife had been found. Maybe Elise really was missing in a traditional sort of way. Why did I jump to the conclusion that she had, in fact, gone missing for nefarious reasons?

The clues were all there. A missing hiker. The full moon. A werewolf on the run. It was all leading me to here. To where, exactly, I didn't know, and soon, it wouldn't matter. In about fifteen minutes, the werewolves of California would be fully transitioned and, from what I knew, out of their minds with blood lust. In fifteen minutes, all of this would be a moot point, unless I saw some sign of Gunther's kill cabin.

And when the sun had gotten to the ten-minute mark, I saw something flash in a valley far below, a valley very nearly hidden beneath a canopy of trees. A flickering flame. I circled it, trying to get a bead on it, but it was mostly hidden at the bottom of two sheer rock walls.

And that's when someone screamed.

I tucked in my great, leathery wings, and dove.

39.

The canopy was too thick for my wingspan.

I alighted, instead, on an overhanging rock that afforded me a view into the narrow valley—and what I saw couldn't have been more strange.

There wasn't just one fire, but many. Most were attached to poles and scattered between the sheer cliff walls. There, to my left and what would be south, was a small cabin. Perhaps the kill cabin, perhaps not. I didn't know.

Most interesting was the massive gate that sealed off entry into the valley—itself about as long as a football field. If I had to guess, the iron gate was a few dozen feet tall. The canyon walls that rose up starkly to the east and west were nearly sheer, difficult to climb, even for the most experienced mountaineer, and probably for a werewolf, too.

Most disturbing were the many, many men who now roamed at the bottom of the valley. All were naked, and all were very, very close to fully transforming into werewolves. I counted eight of them. Unfortunately, my weapon only carried six shots. And there, milling with the others, was Gunther. He, too, was nearly fully transformed. I didn't recognize the others, but I was willing to bet Kingsley would have.

I thought I'd just discovered the source of their reluctance to speak with Kingsley. After all, a good representation of the werewolves of Southern California were here in this valley. My guess was, these were werewolves who preferred to consume live prey, unlike Kingsley who preferred the taste of the rotting and dead.

My eyes caught something else. There, staked to a pole in the center of the valley, was the object of the eight circling, partially-turned werewolves: a woman I could only guess was Elise. Her eyes were closed and she was weeping nearly uncontrollably. I didn't blame her. After all, in a few minutes, she would be dead.

Behind me, out of sight, the sun was nearly set. I had, at best, five minutes.

The valley appeared to open beneath the thick forest canopy, as many of the trees grew straight out from the sheer rock walls. Perhaps there would be room to fly below, I didn't know. But there was no way I was breaking through that tree canopy, not with this wingspan. No, from here, I would have to go at it alone as a human.

I closed my eyes, saw the image of my Samantha Moon self standing in the center of the flame, and a moment later, I was squatting there on the rocks, naked. But I wasn't naked for long. One thing was for damn certain: I wasn't going to fight eight werewolves naked. I dressed in seconds.

Now standing on the rock outcropping, fully clothed and holding the Smith & Wesson .357 Magnum in my right hand, I considered my options. The partially-turned werewolves were much too far for me to squeeze off an accurate shot. Not to mention they were pacing and jumping and clawing the ground and their faces and each other.

They could smell me, too. Already, some of them were sniffing the air, and looking around wildly. The sun was just a minute or so from setting, and I knew what I had to do.

I closed my eyes...and saw the single flame...

40.

A hot wind blasted over me as I focused on the single flame.

Last year, Talos had taught me that even I could go to the moon, using the single flame as a portal. After all, if I could summon him from another dimension, and summon me out of this world and into his, then why I couldn't I summon myself elsewhere? And so I had, and I had frolicked on the moon, no doubt giving one or two unlucky astronomers a heart attack.

Later, I had tested teleporting on earth, and teleported my giant bat self to a snow-covered peak far, far away from here, high in the Alaskan mountains. In fact, I had gone there a few more times, sitting there on an unknown ledge, unseen by human eyes, unexplored, too, no doubt, as I could not imagine any man making his way up there.

But this...this was different. I had never tried to teleport in my human form. In fact, I had never even considered it possible. That is, until I'd seen Dracula himself do it...and he seemed to indicate that I could do it, too.

We'll see, I thought.

The flame was empty for now, flickering there in the forefront of my thoughts...waiting for me to give it a command. Waiting and flickering.

The growling from below intensified. The poor girl had been reduced to whimpering. Why shouldn't she? Here be monsters. Eight of them, in fact. Nine, if you counted me.

Within the flame, I imagined my landing spot, a spot just before the woman chained to the pole. I saw the spot clearly in the flame...and felt myself rush toward it.

When I opened my eyes again, I looked up into the startled face of a weeping woman. Her mouth opened into a scream, and then she did just that: Screamed bloody murder over and over again.

I stood and turned and pointed my weapon at the first creature charging toward me.

41.

My plan wasn't to fight all of them.

Not now, not here. Not like this. And not with only six silver bullets. With eight circling werewolves, the odds weren't in my favor.

No, the plan was to grab her and get the hell out of Dodge.

Or out of this valley of death.

The sun, I knew, was just a few seconds from setting. I knew this as I always knew this, just as the creatures before me knew this, too. We were all slaves to the sun, who was the enemy of the darkness within us. As such, I was always, always aware of its movement through the sky, whether I could see it or not.

All of them were damn close to changing. Most

seemed like they were in excruciating pain.

Except for the one charging me now. Although not fully transformed, he seemed to have the most wits about him. Lucky for me, he'd spotted me almost as soon as I'd appeared.

I had hoped that the precious few seconds I had left of the sunlight could be used to untie the girl and teleport our asses out of here.

Instead, I found myself drawing a bead on the creature charging, the half-man, half were-beast, who ran at me with surprising speed. I could only imagine just how fast they would be once fully transformed.

But these thoughts were fleeting and mostly drowned out by the creature's growl and the woman screaming behind me, as I leveled the gun and aimed for his heart.

And pulled the trigger.

***

The shot was true.

The racing man clutched his chest and lurched forward. His momentum sent him tumbling over the ground. He gasped once, twice, and then lay still. Then, before our very eyes, he transformed back into a naked, middle-aged man. I couldn't see his face, and that was just as well. A very dark and oily shadow rose up from him, swirling, and then the wind seem to catch hold of it, and dispersed it into oblivion. But I knew it wasn't gone. Not entirely. It would wait for another victim, and start its accursed life all over again. It was the way of the dark masters.

I wondered what they thought of a fellow dark master killing their own. That is, until I didn't care what they thought.

I moved around the still-screaming girl and told her to stop screaming. In fact, I quickly reached into her mind to calm her down. Her screaming was making it hard for me to think, and attracting more of the semi-werewolves.

Not that it mattered. Just as I reached out with a pointed index finger, I felt it happen. From one second to the next, I was a different person...and so were the creatures now bounding toward me. They were very, very much different.

The sun had set.

Just like that.

I swiped clean through her ropes and had just reached for her hand, when something powerful hit me from the side...and sent me hurtling head over ass into the grass.

**

I spun to my back and lifted the gun, just as the creature was in mid-leap, its massive, clawed hands reaching for me, its oversized mouth gaping open. The creature was nearly as big as the creature Kingsley had turned into. Nearly, but not quite.

As it flew through the air, I had a clear shot at

its chest, and I took it, simultaneously firing and rolling to my right.

The ground shook with the thudding weight of the beast, who gasped and clawed the earth, and then lay still. As he transformed back into a naked man, I was already up and moving, scrambling back to the now-freed woman.

42.

Six werewolves, all of different sizes and shapes.

Which one had been Gunther, I didn't know, nor did it matter. Not any more.

Six werewolves, four bullets.

The problem was: I couldn't seem to focus long enough on the single flame. I needed a sense of peace around me. Some quiet. The ability to focus.

I could do none of that now as I held the girl's hand and pointed at the circling, hulking, massive creatures that could have just as easily been giant apes or Sasquatches.

For the first time in a long time, I knew I was in a bad situation. There was a chance I could outrun them, although I doubted that. There might even be a chance I could scale this sheer rock wall, or climb the massive gate. But I suspected the werewolves were faster than me.

All of those scenarios involved leaving Elise behind.

And I wasn't going to do that, not now.

I needed to focus to bring forth the single flame, and I couldn't. Not at this moment, and not with these creatures coming closer and closer. They were fearsome, even to me. Each standing well over seven feet tall, some as tall as eight feet. Their heads were huge, as big as a lion's. Their shoulders and arms were thick enough to drag a car behind them. Thick tufts of hair covered each, especially over their chests.

"What's happening?" the girl asked, and just as she asked it, another werewolf charged, one of the smaller ones. I fired and hit him in the neck, and still, he came. I fired again, and hit him just below the heart. Not a direct hit. I fired again and again, until I finally got the fucker in the heart.

He pitched forward, skidding on his face, and when he transformed back to human, I saw that it was Gunther.

Except now, I was out of bullets and we were out of time. To make matters worse, the remaining five werewolves charged at once.

***

They moved fast.

Faster than I could probably run, and certainly faster than I could pull Elise along. There was going to be blood, and it wasn't looking good for either of us.

I had just decided to target the werewolves' eyes —they might be immortal, but they needed to see— when I heard the familiar popping sound.

The man I knew to be Dracula—a man who wasn't really a man, but something else entirely, the first vampire, in fact—appeared before me, brandishing a silver dagger.

Before the closest werewolf could react, Vlad Tepes plunged the blade deep into its chest. As the werewolf pitched forward, Dracula disappeared again with a pop.

The remaining four werewolves appeared confused, although hard to tell through all the fur and the general rage in their eyes. They did, however, pause, and I used that chance to pull Elise away, deeper into the valley.

Behind me, I heard another pop, and turned in time to see Dracula appear behind another werewolf, and drive the silver dagger into its heart from behind.

As it dropped dead, Dracula disappeared again.

Three left, and one of them was gaining on us rapidly, its long stride covering the ground much faster than I could pull Elise along. So, I stopped and did the only rational thing a five-foot, three-inch mother of two would do.

I ran at it as fast as I could, my legs whooshing the air as I built up speed.

Somewhere behind me, I heard another pop as another werewolf howled and thudded to the ground, courtesy of Dracula's blade. Two were left, but I only saw the shaggy beast directly before me. I leaped off my feet, just as it did the same.

43.

Its huge, fur-covered hand caught my fist in mid-strike.

Never had I encountered something so powerful...and this werewolf wasn't even close to being as big as Kingsley was. Its grip was unreal, and its sheer force brought immediate tears to my eyes. It crushed down on my hand, and I felt the bones breaking. It lifted me off the ground and studied me curiously.

I whimpered through the pain and fought his grip to no avail. It brought me closer and I thought that it might look at me more closely, or even smell me, but its mouth opened instead. It was going to take the mother of all bites out of me.

His jaws came at me quickly, rushing at me—and I reverted back to my original plan.

I drove my two fingers deep into his eyes. Hell, I drove them all the way through his eyes and to the back of his skull. The creature howled in pain and tossed me to the side and as it dug its palms into its face, turning in circles, Dracula appeared before him...and drove his dagger deep into his chest. The creature dropped his hands, then dropped to his knees, and pitched forward. A moment later, it reverted back to a middle-aged man with love handles.

This time Vlad didn't disappear, and for good reason. The werewolves were dead, as evidenced by the eight naked men with wounds to their chests. Apparently, Dracula had killed the last while I had been dangling like a fish on a line.

"Are you okay, Samantha Moon?" he asked.

"Yes," I said. "I think."

He wiped the blade in the tall grass, then sheathed it and came over to me, examining my hand. "Nothing that won't heal itself in a few hours. Did he bite you?"

"No, I don't think so."

"Good. Werewolf bites are nasty. They take months to heal, and leave a mark." He pushed up the sleeve of his blood-splattered bowling shirt. Numerous half-moon bite scars criss-crossed his flesh. Apparently, this wasn't Vlad's first rodeo.

We were silent, and I digested what I had just witnessed, had been a part of. Behind me, Elise wept quietly but steadily. The smell of blood was strong in the air. The demoness within me had broken out of my mental cell block, especially at the sight of the Count. I let her be, not wanting to deal with her for now.

She had not approved of the fight. I could tell that immediately. She had not approved of me saving the girl or taking on the werewolves. She had been legitimately concerned for my safety, if only because she didn't want to lose such a valuable host.

Gee, thanks, I thought. *Now keep quiet.*

The blood did not appeal to me. It smelled...tainted somehow. Strange, undesirable.

Vlad must have seen me sniffing and wrinkling my nose. He shook his head. "Stay away from werewolf blood. Their blood, like ours, is mixed with alchemical magic. Some would say dark magic. It would do more harm than good."

Good to know, I thought. Which ruled out me sucking on Kingsley's neck any time soon.

"You killed them," I said.

"You killed them, too, Samantha."

"But I thought...I thought they were your, I dunno, allies."

"Low-level entities tend to favor werewolves, Sam."

"What does that mean?"

"It means, not all are as highly evolved as the entities within us. It means, some of these werewolves were barely journeymen in the dark arts. In fact, it's safe to say that any werewolf who prefers feeding from the living is not very evolved, and they are often a problem. Your werewolf friend, on the other hand, is one of the oldest and most evolved of the lycans."

"He prefers to feed on the dead," I said.

"And so it is with others like him."

"Other evolved werewolves?"

"Right. But there is another reason why I came to your aid, Samantha Moon."

"Because you enjoy killing?"

"Perhaps. Or maybe I fancy you."

"Did Dracula just say he fancies me?"

"He did," said Vlad Tepes. "And now, apparently, he speaks in the third person."

For some reason, I laughed. I never knew Dracula would have a sense of humor...or be heroic. Although his heroism wasn't for altruistic reasons. There was a reason for his noble act...and it was because, well, he *fancied* me.

Unbelievable.

"And, of course, the entity within me more than fancies the entity within you. They were great lovers once, Samantha. They have been lost without each other, until now."

"Well, that's not my problem, and I know where you're going with this...and it's never going to happen. *Ever.*"

Dracula smiled and nodded once. "Nor would I push you to do something that you don't want to do. But perhaps, someday, I can convince you otherwise."

"Don't hold your breath," I said, although that took on a completely different meaning to creatures who didn't breathe.

The Impaler surveyed the surroundings and spied the weeping woman. "You did all of this to save her?"

"Yes."

"You would have died, Samantha Moon."

"Maybe," I said.

He shrugged once and looked again at the woman. I saw a brief flicker of hunger appear in his eyes.

"Don't even fucking think about it," I said.

"I would never take your spoils—"

"She's not my spoils. She's a living, breathing woman that I have every intention of returning safely to her husband."

"Very well, Samantha Moon. Then perhaps this is where I should leave you—"

"Wait!" I said.

He looked at me, tilting his head slightly. He waited.

I said, "How do you keep finding me?"

"Don't you know, Sam?"

"Know what?"

"The entity within me is deeply connected to the entity within you. I can always find you. Always. Just as you can always find me."

"So that was you," I said. "In the sky...the dragon."

He winked...and disappeared.
With a pop.

44.

I wasn't sure this would work, but I tried it anyway. I figured if I could teleport—or apparate—with my clothes on and holding a weapon, I figured I could do the same with Elise.

So, I had her hold me tight around the wrist, then summoned the single flame, and finally envisioned the main highway into town, where there was a sign welcoming tourists. I envisioned the spot just behind the sign.

The pop came again...and it worked much better than I had hoped. When I opened my eyes again, Elise was still holding me tightly, and now we were standing in the shadows of the sign, just a few hundred feet from the town of Arrowhead.

Next, I slipped inside Elise's mind and removed

all her memories of the night. I replaced them with a suggestion that she had been lost for the better part of this day. I told her to count to ten before opening her eyes again, and to head straight into town. I told her to give her marriage another chance and reminded her that her husband loved her deeply.

And then, I was out of her mind and, shortly, amazingly, I teleported myself back inside my minivan, in Gunther's driveway, not entirely sure I hadn't dreamed all of this.

I started the van and drove home.

***

I headed straight to my sister's and gathered up my kids.

I bought two Hot N' Ready pizzas at Little Caesar's on the way home. One for Anthony and one for Tammy and myself.

Once home, I told them they could watch whatever they wanted, just so long as we watched it together. They looked at me funny. Then again, they usually did.

Tammy's hangover was mostly gone, and if I ever thought the words "Tammy's hangover" again, I was going to cry.

In fact, I did cry. With my kids on either side of me, both munching on pizza and with the latest Teenage Mutant Ninja Turtles movie on Netflix, I cried quietly, holding both of their hands, and not releasing them.

Tammy looked at me at some point, obviously wondering what had gotten into her mother, then her eyes widened in horror at what she must have seen in my thoughts. I shook my head slightly and motioned toward the TV.

She set her pizza slice down and curled up next to me, holding my hand tightly.

We would deal with her drinking later. But we would deal with it with love. All the love I have...and then some.

The End

About the Author:

J.R. Rain is an ex-private investigator who now writes full-time. He lives in a small house on a small island with his small dog, Sadie. Please visit him at www.jrrain.com.

Made in the USA
Middletown, DE
09 November 2017